"CHIPS" "JOE"

AND

"MIKE"

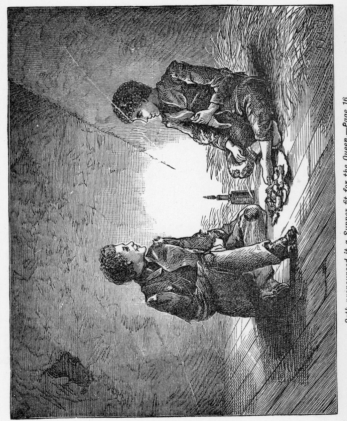

Seth pronounced it a Supper fit for the Queen.—Page 16

"CHIPS" "JOE"

AND

"MIKE"

BY

SILAS K. HOCKING

AUTHOR OF "HER BENNY," "IVY," "ALEC GREEN," ETC. ETC.

WITH ORIGINAL ILLUSTRATIONS

LONDON

FREDERICK WARNE AND CO.

AND NEW YORK

CONTENTS.

CHIPS.

OUR JOE.

7

8 *CONTENTS.*

POOR MIKE.

CHIPS.

CHAPTER I.

SATURDAY NIGHT.

SETH BAKER sat on the floor, trying to rub into his bare feet a sensation of warmth. Seth had been out all the day, and had succeeded in disposing of a tolerably large bundle of chips. It is true that he had met with a great many rebuffs, and night had fallen several hours before he succeeded in parting with his last pennyworth. Still he *had* succeeded, and though he was very tired and very hungry, he had cleared sixpence by the day's transactions, and, as a consequence, was in very good humour with himself, and with the world generally.

It had been a raw, cheerless December day, with

a rising wind, and a sky that had threatened snow since noon. And now, as Seth sat in a corner of his dark windy garret, rubbing his bare feet and listening to the moaning of the wintry wind outside, he fancied he heard also a sound as of snow being sifted on the broken skylight, and falling through to the floor.

It was too dark, however, for him to see anything, and he had no means of getting a light; so he sat rubbing away at his benumbed feet very patiently, giving a low whistle every now and then as the wind, in fitful gusts, went sweeping past.

There was no furniture in the room, not even a fireplace. In the farthest corner from the staircase was a heap of dirty shavings and sawdust, on which Seth and his brother Bob (or Chips, as he was always called) slept at nights; but beyond this there was nothing, if we except an empty ink-bottle, into which the brothers sometimes stuck a candle when they were fortunate enough to get one.

" I wish I had a match," said Seth to himself, at length, " an' I would look about me a bit. But, there! what's the use o' wishin'? If the snow is comin' in, it'll 'ave to come in, for the hole is too high up for us to get at; an' I'll have to wait 'ere till Chips comes, anyhow; but he's precious late, an' I'm nearly clemmed."

Seth might have been nine or ten years of age, certainly not older. He was a bright, intelligent lad, with large dreamy-looking eyes, and a shock of brown thickly-curling hair. His face, however, was pale and very thin, and there was a feebleness about his appearance that seemed ill-fitted for the rough and toilsome life he led.

Seth, however, was not the one to complain. Young as he was, he had already learned that the only way to get on was to take life as he found it, and make the best of it. He had never known any other home than the house in which he then lived. He and his brother had been obliged to shift for themselves ever since he could remember; and though occasionally Chips would speak of another home in which he lived before he came to Bilkey's Court, where there was a piece of carpet before the fire, and a proper bed, in which he slept, and wonderful articles of furniture, the names of which he could not remember, Seth was half disposed to fancy that Chips had dreamed it all, and that he had never known any other home than that in Bilkey's Court. Certainly he could remember nothing of the sort, and so rarely troubled himself about the matter.

And yet to-night, as he sat alone in the cheerless room, with the wintry wind moaning outside, and no light or warmth within, he could not repress a longing that rose in his heart for something brighter and better than he had ever yet known. It was getting on towards bed-time, and yet how would he and Chips be able to sleep on such a night, with hands and feet benumbed with cold, and only shavings and sawdust to keep them warm? He did not know; but he supposed they would manage somehow, as they had managed before. Yet life was very cheerless, and the world to Seth just then seemed very dark and cold.

"I wish there was a meeting on somewhere's," he said to himself at length; "for it's allers warm at meetin's, and I do like to 'ear 'em sing about the 'better land,' as they calls it, an' the beautiful river, and the warmth an' sunshine, and the Saviour as comes to carry us there, if we're only good. My! but if it weren't for leavin' Chips, I wouldn't mind goin' there right away; that I wouldn't." And Seth stopped rubbing his feet, and sat for a long time motionless, staring into the darkness as if he saw something far away beyond the narrow bounds of the dingy room; and something very pleasant, too, for a bright smile spread itself all over his face, and his eyes grew wide with wonder.

"Goodness, now!" said he to himself at length, springing to his feet, "I've been noddin' a bit, I do believe; but that bit of a dream wur 'mazin' nice; but I'll 'av to stir my stumps, or I'll be gettin' cramped."

And Seth began dancing round the room, swinging his arms and beating his sides with his hands at the same time.

"Mercy on us, I forgot it wur Saturday night, an' that there is no fear of the guv'nor and missus turnin' up for long 'nough yet, so I'll 'ave a good turn at jumping while I 'ave the chance. I'm bound to 'ear 'em if they should come in; but, lor'! there's no fear of that, so 'ere goes." And Seth gave a leap in the darkness, alighting on a little snow-drift that had gathered on the floor.

"Oh, Jerusalem!" he ejaculated, "that's a cold 'un, an' no mistake. But 'ere comes Chips, or the guv'nor, or the missus, or the whole lot on 'em together; lor' massy, now, what on earth's up, I wonder?"

And Seth paused to listen. Certainly there was the sound of footsteps on the stairs, but accompanied by a peculiar rustling noise, the like of which he never remembered to have heard before.

"Queer!" he said, scratching his head vigorously, "I can't make it up no road. I've a good mind to shout—I will too, an' risk it."

So leaning over the rail, he shouted down, "Who's there, an' what's yer business?"

"All right, Seth," came the answer, "there's nobody 'bout, is there?"

"No; there's nobody but me. But how are 'e so late, an' what are 'e bringin'?"

"Come and give us a hand, and you'll soon find out," Chips answered; and Seth was soon tugging away at a huge bundle of straw that Chips had brought home with him.

"Oh, glorious!" exclaimed Seth, as soon as he had recovered from his astonishment and delight, "where on earth did 'e get this?"

"I'll tell 'e all about it directly," said Chips, with his head in the straw, and pushing hard behind. And by dint of a good deal of tugging from Seth and pushing by Chips, the straw was at length got up the narrow staircase, and deposited in the corner on the sawdust and shavings. This done, Chips produced a box of matches and a candle, the latter of which was soon lighted, and stuck in the neck of the empty ink-bottle.

"Now, my lad," said Chips, with a comical leer, "look at that an' howl."

"Glorious!" said Seth, stretching himself on the straw and kicking up his heels; "but where did 'e get it, Chips?"

"Chap from the country had a cartful of it," said Chips, "an' was taking it back home again, and so I axes him for a bit. 'How much?' says he. 'Oh, a a handful or two,' says I. 'What for?' says he. 'For me an' Seth to sleep on,' says I; and at that he laughed right out. 'Ain't you got no bed?' says he. 'Only sawdust and shavings,' says I. 'Lor' bless us!' said he, 'thou shalt have as much as thou canst carry.' And at that he twisted a long rope wi' the straw on his thumb in a jiffy. It *wur* curious. I never seen owt like it afore; an' before one could say Jack Robinson a'most, he had tied up all the straw wi' the rope you see there, and hoisted it on my head, an' then, whippin' up his hoss, he drove away, larfin' like anythink."

"He's a brick, anyhow!" said Seth, turning a somer-sault on the straw by way of expressing his delight.

"Right you are," said Chips; "but come, don't you wan't some supper?"

"I did afore you came in," said Seth; "but I'd nearly forgotten all 'bout it."

"Come, then, look alive," said Chips. "I bought a odd lot cheap at the 'Golden Grid,' and there's enough 'ere for to-night and to-morrow also." And Chips produced a miscellaneous assortment of pie-crust, plum-pudding, cold potatoes, bread-crust, bones, and odds and ends of meat of different kinds. Chips was quite right in calling it "a odd lot." But Seth pronounced it a supper fit for the Queen.

" Nothink like variety," said Chips; " I likes a proper assortment when I go in for buying wittles."

Seth made no reply to this remark: he was too busy with his supper to waste time in conversation ; but when the repast was ended, he suggested that if they could stop the hole in the skylight and keep the wind and snow out, " they'd be as snug as the bo'-constrictor in the Z'logical Gardens."

" What 'bout 'im ? " said Chips.

" Why, don't you 'member," said Seth, " how the chap said as how the bo'-constrictor swallered the blanket to keep hissel' warm wi' ? "

" Oh, aye ! " said Chips, " I mind it now; but how about stoppin' yon hole ? "

" Dunno," said Seth ; " it's too 'igh up, I guess. If we had a ladder, now."

" But we ain't," was the reply; " but we can manage, I reckon, arter all."

" Which way ? " said Seth.

" You stand on my shoulders, an' stuff the hole wi' straw."

This was scarcely sooner said than done. ' Splendacious ! " was Chips' remark when Seth had completed the job. And Seth, after regarding it for some time with critical eye, remarked, " That the wind could roar now as much as it liked, and that they, in their new bed of clean warm straw, would be able to listen to it in comfort."

In this Seth was quite right. Long after the candle had burnt itself out the brothers lay in each other's arms, snug and warm, but not at all disposed to sleep. Outside the wind moaned and roared, and tossed the snow about in blinding drifts ; and as they listened to the weird wild music of the storm, they nestled closer together, thankful for their refuge of straw, and more grateful than many a child of wealth screened by damask curtains and covered with quilts of eider-down.

CHAPTER II.

SUNDAY MORNING.

CHIPS was two years older than his brother, and so regarded himself in the light of Seth's protector. Chips was a strong bony lad, with a broad face, large mouth, high cheekbones, and eyes that seemed almost to look through you. Seth might occasionally be duped by the cunning of others, but Chips never was. To outwit Chips Baker in a bargain was what his companions never attempted but once. To outdo him in anything was a feat they rarely accomplished. He was capable of almost any amount of endurance; was swift of foot, strong of arm, and fluent of tongue. Hence Chips was often comparatively well-off while his companions were penniless and hungry.

It was a great trouble to Chips that Seth was so thin and fragile, and very often he wished that he could impart to his brother a little of his own strength. Though Seth never complained, he knew very well that he was often tired almost beyond endurance; and frequently Chips grieved to see that he had little or no appetite for supper, though he had tasted no food since morning. Unfortunately, too, as time went on, he did not seem to get any stronger. On the contrary, if there was any change at all, he got thinner and paler day by day.

Several times during the night in question Chips was disturbed by Seth's cough, and when the feeble rays of the Sabbath morning struggled into the dingy garret, he lay for a long time looking at his sleeping brother, whose face was nestled almost close to his.

" Might 'a been a girl, he's so purty," Chips murmured to himself. " But I wish he wur a bit stronger. But he'll be better when the warm weather comes, I daresay, so it's no use worriting." And with this reflection, Chips nudged him gently with his elbow.

" Well, what's up ? " said Seth sleepily, blinking at his brother out of the corners of his eyes.

" There's a place down in Salford where they're givin' a free breakfas' this mornin'," said Chips.

" An' a meetin' after ? " asked Seth, eagerly.

" I don't know nothin' 'bout no meetin'," said Chips. " All I troubles 'bout is the breakfas'. Will you go ? "

" Aye, that I will," said Seth, jumping up.

' Don't make no noise, if you can help it," said Chips, getting up at the same time. " for if the guv'nor or mother hears us, they'll stop us from goin' out as soon as not, an' search our pockets i' t' bargain."

" Aye, that's so," Seth answered. " But did 'e hear 'em come in last night ? "

" No," said Chips; " an' I didn't sleep for long enough. They must 'a been precious late."

" Guess so ! " said Seth, trying his best to fasten on a pair of worn-out shoes that were at least three sizes too big for him.

" What are 'e after ? " questioned Chips, in a loud whisper.

" Why, I'm trying to fix these 'ere boots," said Seth; " but I'm afear'd it's no go."

" Put some straw in 'em," said Chips, " that'll tighten 'em, and keep yer toes warm at same time."

" Never thought o' it ! " said Seth, proceeding at once to carry out the suggestion, which proved a great success.

" Now, then ! " said Chips, " let's slip out quietly ; but most likely they'll be sleepin' sound enough, for they'd be sartin to be drunk as fiddlers when they got home last night."

This was quite true, for among the inhabitants of Bilkey's Court it had long been the custom for them to go to each other's houses in turn on a Saturday night, after they had been turned out of the public-house. But they were careful not to go empty-handed. Several large jugs were always provided, in which they could take away sufficient beer for another hour's drinking. And sometimes, if money were flush, a pint bottle of gin was also secured, in which case the drunken orgie extended far on into the Sabbath morning.

Among the grown-up population of Bilkey's Court it was held as an undisputed fact that no man could be happy unless he was drunk. Hence the chief ambition of their life was to get drunk as often as possible—not fuddled. No; to be merely "elevated" did not meet the case, but to be thoroughly and completely drunk. Hence many of the men worked industriously and kept sober all the week, so that they might go the whole hog on Saturday night.

John Baker and his wife were among those who believed in enjoying themselves on a Saturday night, whatever might be their experience during the rest of the week. Not that they often remained sober from Sunday to Saturday; for John Baker, as tinplate worker, could earn his thirty shillings a week without difficulty; and Mary, by hiring a sickly baby, and going out begging from door to door, could easily earn another ten shillings; whilst most weeks, by means of threats and abuse, they extorted several shillings from Chips and Seth. So that they managed to get drunk about every third day without much difficulty.

It required a good deal of scheming on the part of Chips and his brother to checkmate their parents, and even then they usually came off only second best. But they bore their defeat, as a rule, very complacently. Kicks and abuse had been a portion of their lot since they could remember, and they scarcely ever hoped for anything better.

They were always on the watch, nevertheless, and kept out of their parents' way as much as possible. Hence their anxiety to get out of the house unobserved on the morning in question; and in this they were successful.

Once in the street, they set off at a quick trot over the crisp sparkling snow. The morning was intensely cold, with a clear frosty sky, and a searching northeast wind that seemed to pierce one through and through.

" Jerusalem ! " muttered Seth, " this are a sneezer, and no mistake ! "

' Aye ! " said Chips. " Christmas 'as come four days too soon; but give us your hand, Seth, and you'll be able to run easier." And hand in hand those two children of want trotted on through the quiet glistening streets, till they were in quite a glow of heat.

" There's the place ! " said Chips at length, pointing to a long low building, around the closed door of which thirty or forty ragged and hungry-looking children were gathered. This number steadily increased, until, by the time the door was opened, a hundred hungry little waifs were trampling the snow, many of them with bare feet, and arms and chests exposed to the keen biting of the wind. They were very patient, however, on the whole; but when at length the door was opened they seemed to surge through in a compact mass.

Inside the temperature was gratefully warm, with a delightful aroma of hot cocoa and buns; and in less time than it takes to write it, they had ranged themselves on the forms in expectant rows, and were impatiently waiting for the good cheer that had been provided.

Several gentlemen and one or two ladies walked up

and down the room to see that all was in order, and to find seats for the late comers. Then one of the gentlemen mounted the platform at the end of the room, and a lady seated herself at an American organ.

"Jerusalem! I wonder what's up now," Seth whispered to Chips, giving him at the same time a nudge in the ribs with his elbow.

But before Chips could answer, the gentleman had rung a little bell, and every eye was strained in his direction.

"Now, boys and girls," he said, "we will sing grace, if you will all stand up. And after that the cocoa and buns shall be handed round, for I have no doubt you are most of you hungry and anxious to begin."

A general nodding of heads greeted this remark, and then the gentleman's voice was heard again giving out the well-known verse :

> "Be present at our table, Lord,
> Be here and everywhere ador'd ;
> Thy creatures bless, and grant that we
> May feast in Paradise with Thee."

The singing was not very good, though Seth thought it delightful, and, hungry as he was, he would gladly have waited to have heard it sung a second time.

Chips, however, had a much keener appetite for food than for music, or, as Seth told him one day, he had a great deal more mouth than ear. Hence Chips was thankful when the singing was over, and lost no time in putting his teeth into the bun when it was handed to him.

It was a pleasantly painful sight, if the paradox

may be allowed. Pleasant to see how thoroughly the poor children enjoyed themselves; painful to look at their pinched haggard faces, and think of their sufferings day by day. More painful still to look on into the future, and wonder what they would become. Many of them would, doubtless, sink beneath the burden of their existence, and, before another winter came, would be laid away to sleep beneath the turf. But others of them would grow up to be men and women—grow up in homes of vice and wickedness, and be surrounded by scenes of infamy and shame. What would they become? There were little children in that company munching greedily at their buns, with round dimpled cheeks and blue innocent eyes, and sweet pouting lips that one almost longed to kiss— little innocents fit to dwell among the angels. What would become of these? Alas! that they should be trampled upon like the snow in the street until they become as foul. If before winter came again they should be sleeping in their graves, who could grieve? Better death than shame a thousand times, for if they live, who shall save them—who?

CHAPTER III.

A GOOD NAME.

"HERE, Chips," said Seth, after he had been munching diligently at his bun for a quarter of an hour, "I can't eat no more; will you have the rest?"

"Nonsents, Seth! you can eat one bun, surely?" said Chips. "I b'lieve I could polish off a dozen on 'em!"

"Then polish off what's left o' mine," was the reply; "for, I tell 'e, I'm licked complete."

"Well, sartinly it's a pity to waste good stuff," said Chips; "so pass it on." And in a trice the remains of Seth's loaf had disappeared down Chip's wide throat.

"Lor, what a mouth!" chuckled Seth, as he watched Chips stowing away the cake.

"Well, what's amiss wi' it?" whispered Chips, with a broad grin.

"Makes me think of what the preachin' gent called it one day," said Seth.

"Well, what's that?"

"A hopen sepulchre!" said Seth, stuffing his fists into his mouth to keep himself from laughing outright at his own wit.

"Why, he didn't mean me, you goose!" said Chips good-humouredly, nudging Seth with his elbow.

"Must a' meaned you," laughed Seth; "for there ain't nobody about that 'as a mouth anywise ekal to it." And Seth laughed again till the tears ran down his cheeks.

"Shut up, you monkey," whispered Chips, playfully nudging him again with his elbow, "the gent's speakin' again."

In a moment Seth was all attention.

"After grace has been sung," said the gentleman, "we shall hold a short service for those of you who are willing or able to stay. No one will be compelled to remain; and yet we shall be glad if all of you will do so."

Whether it was because the room was so cosy, or they remembered the cold wind and snow outside, or whether it was that they thought they would best show their gratitude by staying, certain it is that not ten of them left the room.

"I suppose you have all seen the Manchester Exchange?" said the gentleman, when a hymn had been sung and a short prayer offered.

"Aye, aye! I should think so!" they shouted in chorus.

" Not the inside ? " he asked.

A general shaking of heads greeted that question.

" I thought so," he went on; " and yet I hope you lads, when you get to be men and gentlemen, will do business on the floor of that great building. But I want to tell you that inside that great dome that you have seen from the outside are these words :

" ' A good name is rather to be chosen than great riches '—that is, it is better to have a good name or a good character than lots of money. You haven't any of you much money, and yet, poor as you are, you may all have a good name. Into a neighbourhood in which I once resided there came to live a man and his wife. No one knew who they were, or where they came from ; but as they seemed very respectable people, they were soon invited to their neighbours' houses, and received their visits in return. But after a while it was discovered that the man was a returned convict. He had been a bank manager, and had robbed the bank of a great sum of money, and so was transported ; and when the term of his imprisonment was at an end he came to live with his wife in this neighbourhood, where nobody knew him. But when it got to be known who and what he was everybody shunned him ; he was no longer invited to people's houses, or treated as he had been before, and he was glad enough to get away to some other place, where his character was not known. You see, boys and girls, he had lost his good name, and got a bad one instead. So that if you would have a good name, you must be honest.

" I read a story some time ago of a little boy who, playing marbles one day with some other boys, stole one of the marbles and put it into his pocket, and as the lad from whom it was stolen had a great many marbles, he did not miss it. After a while the lad stole a cake from his mother, out of a cupboard, and she did not miss that. So he got bolder, and stole some money from his father, and spent it in oranges and spice, and his father did not miss the money ; so he thought he might go on stealing without ever being found out. After a while he got into a milliner's shop as errand-boy, and in time he had to help to serve behind the counter. So he began taking money out of the till : at first a very few pence, then more and more. At length he was detected, and transported —sent across the ocean—and never saw his parents or friends again. Now, you see, all that came out of stealing a marble. Now, I want you who mean to be honest to hold up your hand."

In an instant up went a forest of hands.

"That's right," continued the gentleman. "And I want you to remember also that if you would have a good name, you must be sober also. In other words, don't drink. 'Drunkard' is a very bad name, but no boy or girl need be ashamed of being called a teetotaller.

In the next place, if you would have a good name, you must be truthful. People who tell lies always get found out sooner or later, and then nobody will believe them, even when they speak the truth.

"I see some of you are getting sleepy, so I will tell you a funny story I heard some time ago. A lad, finding both his father and mother out, thought he would make some toffee for himself, so he stole some butter and sugar out of the cupboard, and soon had it boiling in a pan quite ready to pour out. He thought, however, that he had better first see if the coast were clear, so he ran to the door and looked out, and was very much terrified to see his father coming along the street. What to do he did not know. The boiling hot toffee would have to be poured somewhere out of sight, and that quickly ; and at length, in desperation, he poured it into his trousers' pocket. When his father came into the room he was jumping about as if the floor were hot. ' What's the matter, Jack ? ' said his father ' Nothing—nothing; oh, dear ! ' he cried. ' But there must be something wrong,' said his father. ' No, there isn't,' he said. ' Oh, dear ! oh, dear ! oh, dear ! ' And then he had to confess all about it."

For some time after this the laughter was so great that nothing more could be said. When, however, it had subsided a little, the gentleman went on again.

" You see, boys and girls, that wrong-doing always brings its own punishment. Always be honest; always tell the truth. And I want you to be kind also, and industrious and persevering.

" You will find it hard work to be good sometimes —we all do—but if we trust in Jesus, He will help us. We sing sometimes, 'Look ever to Jesus; He'll bring you safe through.' Years ago, when there were slaves in America, the poor slaves tried sometimes to make their escape to Canada. They knew if they could get there they would be free, but they knew nothing about the way. All they knew was that it was due north, and that if they would follow the pole star they would get there in time, unless they were captured or died on the road. So off they would start, travelling chiefly through the night, over hedges and bridges, swimming rivers and wading through swamps, but always keeping the pole star in view, until they crossed the river that divided the two countries; then they were free. Well, boys and girls, if we would be good and find our way to heaven, the better land, we must look to Jesus. He is our pole star, our only hope, our only Saviour. I heard of a wicked father that used to flog his little boy for going to church, but he could not flog away his love for Jesus. The little fellow used to sell apples at a railway station, and one day he fell on the line, and the train went over both his legs. He asked the doctor who was dressing his horrible wounds:

"'Doctor, shall I get better?'

"'No, my poor boy,' said the doctor; 'you are dying now.'

"'Then,' said he, with a faint smile, 'tell 'em at home I died a Christian.' And so he passed away.

"It was Jesus that helped him to be good and brave and to die in the faith of the Gospel, and He will help you, every one of you, to be good if you will trust in Him. Pray to Him for strength every night and morning, and He will comfort and help you here, and by and by take you to His beautiful home in heaven. Now, before you go home, we will sing together one more hymn. It is called, 'When Jesus comes.'"

Seth could only remember the last verse, but that he never forgot, and many times during the next few days he repeated the words over again and again to himself:

> " He'll know the way was dreary,
>   When Jesus comes;
> He'll know the feet grew weary,
>   When Jesus comes ;
> He'll know what griefs oppressed me,
>   When Jesus comes ;
> Oh, how His arms will rest me !
>   When Jesus comes."

Seth thought that morning the happiest of his life. " Chips," he said, as they journeyed homewards through the snow, " I mean to die a Christian."

" Do you ? " said Chips.

" Aye, that I do," he said earnestly ; " though," he added, with a bright roguish smile, " I don't intend to die yet awhiles."

" I should think not," said Chips reflectively ; " we may get well-off in time ; who knows ? "

" We shall all be well-off in the ' better land,' " said Seth, looking serious again. " I do like to hear 'em sing and talk about Jesus an' heaven an' all the other nice things."

" Well, for my part," said Chips, " I'd rather 'ave a good feed than all the singin' i' t' Manchester."

Seth made no reply to this, and the rest of the way they journeyed in silence. They received only abuse when they got home, but the peace in Seth's heart did not pass away ; and when he laid his tired head upon the straw that night, he somehow felt happier than he had done for many a day before.   He did not talk much, but Chips heard him repeating **to** himself just before he dropped off to sleep—

> " Oh, how His arms will rest me !
>   When Jesus comes."

CHAPTER IV.

CHRISTMAS EVE.

FOR the next three or four days Chips and Seth followed their usual employment, though with varying success. Chips generally managed to dispose of his bundle by dark; but Seth was not such a good salesman. If to the question, "Any chips to-day, mum?" he received the answer, "No, my lad," he would turn away without another word. But Chips, on the contrary, would have his bundle on the door-step in a moment, and would open a conversation something to the following effect:

"Not to-day, mum? Well, now, that *is* unfortunate. These chips I has is special good ones; I selected 'em myself, and can guarantee 'em all sound, mum. 'You 'ave some already?' just so, mum, but chips is always wanted, an' these 'll keep, mum; an' I don't know when I may 'ave such a good lot again. 'How do I sell 'em?' well, mum, generally I sells twelve bundles for a penny, but as it's you, mum, an' Christmas-time, I'll say thirteen as twelve. I can't afford to do it as a general thing, mum, but as the gents say at the big shops, I want to clear out surplus stock. 'An old hand,' am I, mum? Well, you see, I has to get my own livin' in an honest way, mum, and I'm quite sartin you'll find these chips all I says, mum. 'Two pennorth,' you say? Yes, mum, thirteen as twelve; I stick to my word, mum. A threepenny bit this" (putting the coin into his mouth). "You may as well take another pennorth: there you are, mum; saves the trouble of givin' change, you see. Good evenin', mum, and much obliged." And Chips would doff his cap, and walk away with an air of great satisfaction.

Meanwhile poor little Seth would be tramping from door to door, his bundle growing very little lighter as the day wore away. Sometimes Chips would go in search of Seth when he had disposed of his own stock, and if he were fortunate enough to find him, would give Seth a few lessons in the art of "chip-selling," for which the little fellow would be very thankful, though he never profited very much by it.

On the afternoon of Christmas Eve, Chips and Seth started from the timber-yard (where they were allowed by the foreman, who knew them well, to gather up what odds and ends of broken wood they could find) in different directions. Seth had been very poorly all the day. At breakfast-time he had scarcely been able to eat a morsel of food, and at dinner-time his appetite was no better, so that when he started on his journey he was so weak that he could scarcely drag one leg after another. He tried his best, however, to carry out Chips' advice, and "keep a stiff upper lip;" but it was very hard work, and he thought he had never felt so weary before in his life. To make matters worse, the wind blew against him in strong fierce gusts, and the cold was almost more than he could bear.

"It's no sort of use," he said to himself at length, 'I can't manage it no road to-day, so I'll go home, and lie down a bit; maybe I'll feel better after restin' a bit."

Fortunately Bilkey's Court was not far away, and dropping his bundle of chips at the foot of the stairs, he clambered up into the dingy garret, crept across on his hands and knees to his refuge of straw, and lay down, utterly exhausted, and completely out of heart. He felt very much better after a while, though he had no thought of venturing out again for that day.

The day was rapidly drawing to a close when his father came home hungry and excited. He had quarrelled with his master and had been dismissed, and, as a consequence, he was ready to quarrel about anything or with anybody.

"Hallo!" he exclaimed, stumbling over Seth's bundle of sticks; "what's the meaning o' this?"

"Seth's poorly," replied his wife, "an' is gone up to lie down."

"Don't believe a word of it," he growled. "The

young vagabond is only skulking. I'll soon teach him another lesson." And going to the foot of the stairs he shouted, " Seth, come down this minute; d'ye hear ? or if you don't, you'll wish you had."

"Yes, father," said the little fellow meekly. And a minute later Seth stood before him, trembling and tearful.

"What d' ye mean skulking in this manner, you young dog ? " said his father, grasping him rudely by the shoulder.

"I didn't think it was skulkin', father," said Seth; "only I felt very poorly. But I'm better now."

"And it's quite time you were, I can tell you," said his father, striking him on the side of his head with his hard open palm, and sending him staggering against the wall. "Now, pick up that bundle this minute and be off with you, and don't dare show your face here until you've sold every stick; and mind you bring the money back with you also."

"Yes, father," said Seth tearfully. And the next minute he had shouldered the heavy bundle, and had gone forth into the cold wintry street.

An hour later Chips returned quite white with snow, and was allowed to sit by the fire down-stairs in consideration of the fact that he handed over to his father all his money.

" Is Seth home ? " Chips asked at length.

"No," said his mother. "He 's been home, but as he hadn't sold his chips, his father sent him off again an hour ago, and told him not to come home until he had sold the lot." Saying which, she followed her husband out of the house; for it was Christmas Eve, and they had arranged for a carousal in honour of the occasion.

Chips was frightfully indignant at the treatment Seth had received, and sat for a long time staring into the fire, with an angry frown upon his brow. Outside the wind roared and wailed, and tossed the snow against the windows, and whistled through the keyhole, and rattled the badly-fitting door; and as Chips listened his anger blazed forth, and he began stamping round the room like a caged lion.

If there was anything in the world that Chips loved it was Seth. Perhaps he loved him all the more because he had nothing else to love. Seth was everything to him, and Chips was never happier than when the cheerful little fellow was poking fun at him or chaffing him, as he so well knew how to do. Chips was never angry with him. Angry! Chips would have been indignant at the suggestion. How could anyone be angry with little Seth?

And yet now, this wild winter's night, this evening of all evenings in the year, when children should be safe and snug at home, when in the homes of the rich the little ones would be enjoying themselves with music, and dance and song, his little Seth—his little fragile brother—was out in the storm and snow, with no one to help him, or pity, or bless.

" If I only knew where to find him," said Chips to himself, " I would start this blessed minnit. But I *don't* know—that's the rub; an' how tired an' cold the poor little chap will be!" And Chips proceeded to replenish the fire. " I'll 'ave a good fire for him 'gin he comes home," he muttered, " though father a'most kills me for burning the coal." And Chips drew up a rickety chair against the fire, and sat down, with a heavy heart, to wait the return of his brother.

As the evening wore away his anxiety increased : one hour after another he heard struck by the clock of a neighbouring church, and still Seth came not. What could be the reason ? Surely he had not come home and crept up to the garret without his hearing him ? At any rate, he would make sure. And Chips lighted a candle and bounded quickly up the garret stairs, and across to the bed of straw. But Seth was not there, and with a groan he turned away and slowly retraced his steps. When the clock struck the hour of midnight Chips could sit still no longer, he felt ready to choke. Something had happened to his little brother, there could be no doubt whatever. Perhaps he had been run over ; or perhaps he had dropped dead in the snow—who could tell ? "And here I be," moaned Chips, wringing his hands, "without a bit of a chance of helping the little chap."

And Chips went out and stood in the open doorway, and looked up and down the silent court. The snow was still falling, and the night wind was bitterly cold, but Chips did not heed it. All his thought was for little Seth. Where was he this wild, solemn night ? Was he crying somewhere alone in the dark, with no one to help ? Or was he beyond the cold and pain in the "better land," of which he was so fond of speaking ?

"Oh that I could *do* some'at !" he moaned, looking out into the dark court with white anguished face.

Then it suddenly occurred to him that perhaps he

could pray about it. It was true, he had never prayed in his life; but at the meetings he had attended he had heard the gentleman speak about prayer, and how the Lord Jesus heard them, and would help them when they were in trouble and difficulty.

"I can try, anyhow," said Chips to himself. And he went out and knelt down in the snow, and, looking up into the dark wintry sky, he clasped his hands together, and said:

"O Lord Jesus, please do look after little Seth. I don't know where he is; but if You come across him anywhere, please give him a lift. He's been poorly all day, and father never ought to 'a sent 'im out. I'm afraid it 'll be a case wi' him, unless You take him in hand. Oh, please do just look him up, an' keep him safe an' warm till mornin'. Amen."

Somehow Chips felt all the better after giving expression to his trouble in this way; and he was not without a hope that the Lord Jesus would answer his prayer. He was still watching in the open doorway when his parents reeled home, and, at the stern bidding of his father, crept silently up into the dark lonely garret, and lay down on the straw to wait and watch for the morning. It was the first night he could ever remember being without his little brother, and it seemed very strange and desolate. Besides, there was a great fear in his heart lest his little Seth should never more share his bed of straw, and so he lay, staring with glassy eyes into the darkness, and starting at every sound that broke the stillness of the night. Scores of times, as the solemn hours dragged slowly away, he fancied he heard Seth's footstep on the stairs, and would start up and listen; then, with a sigh, he would lie down again to fancy anon, as the wintry wind wailed around the house, that he heard his feeble voice crying in the darkness for succour and help.

Such a night as that poor Chips had never known before. Yet it came to an end at length; and just as the day was breaking, worn-out with watching and anxiety, he dropped off into a dreamful and troubled sleep.

CHAPTER V.

CHRISTMAS DAY.

WHEN Chips awoke it was broad day, and the air was full of the wild melody of Christmas bells. For a moment he seemed bewildered, feeling sure that something had happened, but unable to recall what. Then suddenly the recollection of the drear night he had passed through came back to him, and, burying his face in the straw, he moaned, " O Seth, Seth, my little Seth, please do come home to me, or I'll break my heart!"

Then for the first time he gave way to tears. "Oh, what shall I do?" he wailed, the tears streaming down his cheeks. "What shall I do without my little Seth? If Seth is dead, I hope I'll die too."

Then raising his eyes towards heaven, he cried out in agony, "O Lord! if You do care a bit for us—I mean us who are poor, an' 'ave nobody to help us—then jist take care of little Seth, and I'll never be glad enough as long as I live."

After a while he grew calmer, and hearing his father and mother moving about in the room below, he crept silently down the stairs and into their apartment.

"Oh, father!" he burst out, "Seth's never been in for the night."

"An' who cares for that?" was the savage reply.

"Don't *you* care?" asked Chips in astonishment.

"Not I, indeed," was the answer. "I'd be glad if the both of you were dead and buried."

For a moment Chips looked at him, his face flushing with anger and shame; then turning to his mother, he said, "And don't you care, mother?"

"Don't bother me," she answered, "the brat'll turn up all right, never fear."

"They can't be sober," was Chip's thought, "or they'd never talk in that way;" and turning on his heel, he strode out of the house. The Christmas bells were still swinging out their music on the wintry air, but to Chips they brought no feeling of mirth or gladness; they might sound joyously to those whose hearts were glad, but not to him. He only heard one deep tone in the chimes that sounded like a knell; he had heard it at funerals, he heard it now, sounding distinct and solemn above all the rest.

It was yet comparatively early, and the great city seemed almost asleep under its white canopy of snow. Chips wondered, as he hurried down Shude Hill, that there were so few people abroad, and when he got into Market Street his wonder increased. A few solemn policemen were moving hither and thither, tracking the white carpet under their feet; but they were about the only visible signs of life.

"I can't make it up no road," said Chips to himself. "Bells a-ringin' an' nobody about! What's up, I wonder?"

Poor Chips! In his grief and anxiety he had forgotten that it was Christmas Day. He had hoped, when he left home, that he would meet with some newspaper boys of his acquaintance, and get to know from them if there was anything in the papers about any boy having been lost, or run over, or killed; hence he was greatly disappointed at finding nobody about.

For a long time he stood at a street-corner, wondering what he should do next. Then it suddenly occurred to him that perhaps Seth had got hurt, and had been taken to the infirmary.

" I'll go and see, any'ow," he said, bounding up Market Street at a rate that almost astonished himself.

" Hullo, Chips Baker! what's up?"

It was a lad of Chip's acquaintance who spoke.

" Is that you, Bill?" said Chips, glad to meet with anyone whom he knew.

" Aye, it's me; or, leastways, I thinks it are. But what's up?"

" Seth's lost," said Chips, lowering his voice. " Father sent him out 'esterday aft'noon, and he's never comed home. What can it mean, Bill?"

" No knowin'," said Bill. " An' bein' Christmas, there'll be no gittin' to know, I 'spect."

" Aye; it's Christmas, ain't it? I'd clean forgot all 'bout it," said Chips. " Still, if he's got hurt, they may know some'at 'bout it at the 'firmary. At any rate, I'll ax; so 'ere's off."

But disappointment still dogged his steps. Nobody answering to the description he gave of Seth had been brought in, and, with a sigh, he turned away to prosecute his search elsewhere.

Passing a church later on in the day, the door of which stood open, he crept inside. He had no particular object in doing so, only he was tired and cold, and almost heartbroken; and he was utterly at his wits' end to know what to do or where to go, and he thought—for hope had almost died out of his heart—that he would be as likely to find Seth in a church as anywhere else. The congregation had just commenced to sing as he crept noiselessly and unobserved into an empty pew and seated himself on a hassock, so that he might be out of sight. He thought he had never heard such singing before, and the music of the organ was wonderfully sweet. The words, too, somehow seemed very comforting to him just then, and he could not help thinking how Seth would enjoy it if he were there.

> "Art thou weary, art thou languid,
>   Art thou sore distressed?
> 'Come to Me,' said One; and coming,
>   Be at rest.
>
> "If I still hold closely to Him,
>   What hath He at last?
> 'Sorrow vanquished, labour ended,
>   Jordan passed.'
>
> "If I ask Him to receive me,
>   Will He say me nay?
> 'Not till earth and not till heaven
>   Pass away.'"

Chips could not make it all out, but he was satisfied that it referred to the "Lord Jesus." He had heard something before about "coming to Him, and being at rest," but it was not very clear to him yet.

Then came the sermon, and Chips heard, for about the second time in his life, the story of the Angels and the Shepherds, and the Saviour who was born in Bethlehem of Judea; he heard, too, about the miracles of healing He wrought, the loving words He spoke, and the beautiful home in heaven He had prepared for all those who loved and served Him. And Chips wondered " whether this good Saviour had taken Seth to the better country ? whether, with his little brother, the ' Jordan was passed,' and he had found the everlasting rest ? " From what the preacher said, this Saviour was more loving than anyboby else in the world, and in the home He had fitted up there would be no hunger, nor cold, nor pain, nor poverty, nor sickness, nor death for ever. And Chips thought that if Seth were really dead, and gone to Jesus, he was a lot better off; that he was away out of the reach of the wind and snow, and that he had found a Friend who would love him and take care of him for ever.

And yet, as Chips thought of these things, bitter silent tears trickled down his cheeks, and great sobs shook his frame.

" I oughtn't to fret," he said to himself, " if Seth's better off, but I can't help it,—he's all I has to love."

Chips crept out of the church just before the service concluded, and waited in the street till all the people came out; but little Seth was not amongst them, and with a great sob he turned away. He had tasted no food for the day, and was almost faint, but he never once thought of himself. If he could only find his brother, he would not mind going without food for a week. So up and down the cheerless streets he tramped hour after hour, resolved not to give up his search while there was daylight left in the sky. But it was all to no purpose. Of all the people he spoke to, not one of them could give him any information respecting his brother. So when at length the last glimmer of day had disappeared, he stole away to Bilkey's Court. His heart was well-nigh breaking, and he thought it would do him good to get away to his own dark corner and weep alone.

As he neared his home, hope revived within him for a few minutes. " It might be," he thought, " that Seth had come home during his absence." And with quickened steps he pressed forward, though his strength was all but gone.

At the door of the " living room," as it was called, he paused for a moment and listened ; but no sound came from within, and pushing open the door, he found it empty. The next moment he was bounding up the garret stairs. At the top he paused again. Yes, there could be no doubt about it, he heard something moving in the straw : " his lost brother had come home," was his thought, and with a low cry of " Seth, Seth ! " he sprang toward the bed. As he did so, something rushed swiftly past him and disappeared in the darkness ; but without heeding it he dropped on his knees on the floor, and stretched his hands out over the straw bed, expecting to find his own little Seth ; but Seth was not there, and with a groan that might have been heard in the next street, he fell prone upon the floor.

How long he lay there he never knew ; but when he crept into his bed of straw, the warm place where the cat had been sleeping had grown cold again, and not a single sound broke the awful stillness of the night. Chips had given up hoping for Seth's return now.

"He'll never come 'ome no more ; oh, he'll never come 'ome no more ! " he sobbed, " my little Seth ! my little Seth ! " And so he lay throughout the night, rolling his head from side to side, and calling, in an agony of grief, the name of his little brother.

Chips never forgot that Christmas-tide. Years after he spoke of it with eyes brimful of tears : spoke of it as the bitterest drop in the bitter cup of his life, and wondered how he lived through those long hours of suspense.

If he had been certain that poor little Seth was dead and out of all his misery, he would have sobbed himself to sleep. But the awful uncertainty that shrouded his fate banished all hope of slumber, and compelled him to lie wakeful, suffering the acutest torture he had ever known. And when morning dawned at last, he stole silently down the stairs, with pale haggard face and wild bloodshot eyes, and plunged again into the wintry streets, to commence anew his search.

CHAPTER VI.

A DREAM OF HEAVEN.

WHEN Seth left his home — his father's threat ringing in his ears — and wandered forth into the fast-gathering darkness, he had no idea what direction he should take, and little hope of disposing of his burden. For a long time he wandered on quite aimlessly, keeping as much as possible on the sheltered side of the streets, but utterly indifferent to—and, indeed, unconscious of— the direction he was taking. The wind was very boisterous, and the snow almost blinded him sometimes; but still he pushed on in a dazed hopeless kind of way. His hands and feet were benumbed with cold, but in his head a fire seemed to burn, and on his heart a weight infinitely heavier than the burden on his back.

D

He had a vague half-defined idea that he had been wronged,—that he ought not to have been driven forth into the wind and snow, weak and ill as he was,—yet he had no thought of disobeying his father.

Chips would have hid the bundle somewhere until the morrow, and invented some kind of story with which to satisfy his father. But Seth was of different calibre, both physically and morally. So he plodded on through the blinding snow, going away before the wind as much as possible, until he discovered that he had got beyond the neighbourhood of shops, and was in a locality given up to private residences; but whether he was at Cheetham Hill or Brooke's Bar he seemed to have no idea. That matter, however, did not trouble him; to dispose of his burden was now his only business. So he went up timidly to the first door of a long terrace of handsome houses, and then to the second and third, and so on to the end, and in every instance the answer was the same; that is, when the person who answered the door deigned to speak to him, for in many instances the door was slammed abruptly in his face before he had time to speak.

In some of the houses he heard the sound of music and laughter, for the young people were making merry on Christmas Eve, little dreaming of the poor little shivering lad who was being rudely spurned from their door.

In the last house—as he was turning away—he heard the sound of singing, and paused again to listen. It might be that they were singing Seth's favourite hymn, or it might be that his own imagination supplied the words, but surely enough he heard them :

> " He'll know the way was dreary,
>   When Jesus comes ;
>   He'll know the feet grew weary,
>   When Jesus comes.

> " He'll know what griefs oppressed me,
>   When Jesus comes ;
>   Oh, how His arms will rest me !
>   When Jesus comes."

" Aye," he said, a smile spreading itself over his pale face, " it's very nice. I think I'll rest 'ere a bit an' listen. It don't seem as cold as it did when I started, so I'll be all right for a bit."

So he crept under the window, and throwing his bundle of chips on the ground, sat on them in a listening attitude. The snow was still falling, and the wind made strange weird music in the bare trees that grew all along the terrace, which Seth mistook sometimes for the music within ; but the feeling of cold and hunger had passed away, and on his face there was an expression of perfect content.

At length the sound of laughter fell on his ears, and he got up and crept close to the window. The blind was not quite down at one corner, and Seth could not resist the temptation of taking a peep within. He never considered whether it was right or proper. He had no wrong in his heart, so he stood there holding to the ledge of the window with his almost frozen hands, and devouring, with great hungry eyes, the bright picture within.

On the floor was a thick spongy carpet of warm

cheerful colours, and on the walls hung beautiful pictures, set (in what Seth thought) were frames of gold. A bright fire was blazing in the polished grate, flinging its cheerful ruddy glare across the room, while beautiful and well-dressed boys and girls were seated in the soft roomy chairs, or were moving gracefully up and down the handsome apartment.

Such a picture Seth had never seen before in his life. Oh, what bliss he thought it would be to lie on the shaggy rug before that blazing fire ! Could heaven be a brighter place than that room within ? he wondered, or could the angels be prettier or happier than those boys or girls ? Certainly he could conceive of nothing brighter or more beautiful.

After a while he noticed all the children gather in a circle round the piano, while a beautiful girl, with long golden hair, sat down and commenced to play. Seth fairly held his breath to listen. It was not " When Jesus comes " this time, but something he had never heard before. Very distinctly the words fell on his ear, warbled forth by the pure childish voices within :

> " While shepherds watched their flocks by night,
>   All seated on the ground,
> The Angel of the Lord came down,
>   And glory shone all round.

> " ' Fear not,' said He (for mighty dread
>   Had seized their troubled mind) ;
> ' Glad tidings of great joy I bring
>   To you and all mankind.' "

Seth did not understand very clearly what it meant, yet it was so sweet that he thought he could listen all night; and very sorry he was to see all the children at length leave the room, while a minute later a servant came in and put down the lights.

Creeping back to his bundle of sticks, he sat down again. He thought the children would come back again directly. Indeed, in a very few minutes they had come back, or at any rate Seth thought they had; for he heard again the tones of the piano, and the children's voices chanting the much-loved words:

> " Oh, how His arms will rest me !
> When Jesus comes."

But it might have been only the sighing of the cold wind in the trees, and the echo of the song that yet lingered in his heart.

He did not go to the window again. He felt so warm and restful where he was that he had no wish to move. He had slipped unconsciously to the ground and lay half - buried in the snow, with his head upon the chips, and a sweet smile playing round the corners of his mouth.

He had forgotten by this time all about the errand on which he had come—forgotten his father's anger and his own weakness. There was music all around him, and the white silent snow that was so gently covering him felt soft and warm. The fire that burned in his brain had passed away, and the weight upon his heart had gone. It was all peace now, and rest and content.

It was all dark around him at first, but after a while the darkness too began to pass away, and the music that sounded as if from far in the distance, began to come nearer and nearer, growing sweeter all the while. And, strangest of all to him, the wall of the house began to melt and vanish, and the beautiful room he had seen began to stretch itself out in all directions, until he found himself in the centre of a very fairyland of beauty. And the flowers in the carpet lifted up their heads and began to live, and the golden frames of the pictures became the gateways to other scenes of loveliness that stretched away as far as eye could reach, and instead of a dozen or twenty children, there were hundreds, dressed in the most beautiful raiment he had ever seen, and carrying in their hands the loveliest flowers; and as he lay there wondering at all he saw, one of the children came and touched him, and said in a voice sweeter than any music he had ever heard, " Come, Seth, will you not join us, for it is morning now ? " And Seth got up and looked around him, and, lo ! all the darkness had passed away, and the trees were no longer bare, but covered with the most beautiful leaves, and in the distance there rolled down a river, with water clear as the clearest glass, and on its sunny banks hundreds of happy children were at play.

Seth thought he would very much like to join them ; but how could he ? He was only a poor chip-boy, and his clothes were dirty and torn. And yet suddenly he found himself upon its brink and looking down into its clear crystal depths, in which he saw the reflection of himself. Could it be possible ? Certainly it was his own face ; for he had looked at himself many times in shop windows, and recognized himself again without difficulty. But his clothes were no longer dirty or torn; on the contrary, he was dressed like the other children in the most beautiful attire.

"Well, this is nice," said Seth, turning to his companion. "I never had so nice a dream before. I should like it to last for ever."

"And your wish shall be granted," said his companion.

And all the children began to sing as they gathered round him, till the air was full of music again; and in the trees above his head there was a rush as of angels' wings, and the snowflakes fell silently still. But Seth did not know it now.

There he lay, with his head upon the chips, a happy smile upon his face, and his eyes wide open; and still the snow came down like feathers from angels' wings, and gently covered up his white gentle face, and hid his rags from human gaze. And so at the last little Seth Baker, the chip - boy, was clad in white raiment, and had gone home to die no more.

An hour later carriages were driven up to the gate, and as the children tripped down the garden path to the carriages that were waiting, they said to each other, "Only look! See how the snow has drifted under the window! Did you ever see such a curious drift?"

They did not know that little Seth was sleeping there. It was well, perhaps, they did not know, for he was beyond their succour and compassion now, and was better off than they.

In their downy beds they fell asleep, and awoke in the morning to the sound of Christmas bells, while Seth, from his bed of snow, woke up to the music of heaven, and to the joy that would last for ever.

CHAPTER VII.

A REVELATION.

"HI, Dick, is there owt in the paper this mornin' about Seth, do 'e think?"

"Dunno, Chips," answered the news-boy; "but there's some'at on the pla-card 'bout somebody found dead i' t' snow."

"Oh, dear!" said Chips, turning pale. "I wonder if it is Seth?"

"Caan't say," said the boy; "but 'ere's a paper; read it for yoursel'."

Just then a gentleman came up and bought a paper, and was turning away when Chips touched him on the arm.

"If you please, sir," he said, "will you read in the paper what's said 'bout somebody found dead in the snow, for I'm fear'd it's my little brother."

" I shall be sorry if it's your brother," said the gentleman, opening out the paper and searching for the paragraph. " Oh, here it is ; " and he commenced to read, while Chips listened with eyes and mouth wide open.

" ' Yesterday morning as Mr. Maclaver and family, of Rodney Terrace, Victoria Park, were leaving their home for church, they noticed what seemed a peculiarly shaped snow-drift under their drawing-room window. On the snow being removed, however, a lad of eight or nine years of age was discovered, quite dead, with his head resting upon a bundle of chips. The body was at once removed to the " Friendship Inn," where it awaits identification. An inquest will be opened to-morrow morning.' "

During the reading of the above brief paragraph Chips had grown as pale as a sheet, and when the gentleman had finished, he stood for several seconds as if transfixed, his eyes seeming almost to start out of his head.

" Are that all ? " he gasped at length.

" Yes, my lad ; that's all. Do you think it is your brother ? "

" Aye, it's Seth, sure 'nough," he said, with a great gulp. The next moment he had pulled off his tattered shoes, and was bounding along Mosley Street at the speed of the wind.

He had tasted no food for thirty-six hours, and was almost faint from exhaustion ; but he did not realize his weakness. He felt neither hunger nor cold. He only knew that his worst fears were realized—that his little Seth was dead.

During the reading of the above brief paragraph Chips had grown as pale as a sheet

On, on, he went, the snowy pavement seeming to fly from beneath him. He did not notice that people stared at him as he passed——he heeded nothing that was passing around him. One all-consuming desire prevaded his entire being. All else was forgotten.

The " Friendship Inn " was easily found. Yet when Chips stood before the landlord he was unable to speak for several seconds.

" Well, boy, what is it ? " said the landlord.

But Chips only stared at him, gasping the while for breath.

" Why, what in the world is the matter with the boy ? " said the landlord.

Then the words came in convulsive gasps. " You 'ave a little boy 'ere brought in from the snow ? "

" Yes, my lad. Do you know who he is ? "

" My brother, I 'spect; may I see 'im ? "

" Yes, come this way ; we are anxious for the body to be identified."

Up a flight of stairs, along a narrow passage, and into a large empty room Chips followed his conductor.

" There he is," said the landlord, pointing to a corner of the room, where, on the floor, a little figure lay outlined under a white sheet.

In a moment Chips was kneeling beside the prostrate figure. Then turning his beseeching eyes toward the landlord, he gasped, " I can't do it, sir ; I can't do it."

" Can't do what ? " said the landlord.

" I can't pull off the coverin'; will you do it, please ? "

" Oh, yes," said the landlord, instantly complying with the request.

The next moment Chips was gazing at his little brother, whose pale sweet face was stiffened in the last long sleep.

Chips did not cry or start, or make a movement of any kind. There he crouched on his hands and knees as though he had been changed into stone, gazing with hungry eyes at the cold placid face that never again would beam upon him with smiles of welcome.

But for the deathly pallor one might have thought little Seth asleep. There was nothing repulsive about the calm set face. His eyes were closed now, but about the slightly-parted lips you could almost fancy a smile yet lingered, while every line of want and pain had been smoothed away by the cold hand of death. It would seem as though he had died without a struggle, or had been lulled to sleep by the music of the wind, and by the songs of happy children.

As Chips did not move nor speak, the landlord went away and left him, and returned again in half an hour, to find Chips wiping away his own tears from the pale face of the dead, and moaning to himself, "O Seth, Seth! will you never speak to me no more? Don't you know me, Seth? I'm Chips, your brother Chips. O Seth, Seth, my little Seth!"

The landlord was so touched by the boy's grief that he led him away at length, and gave him food, and did his best to comfort him.

John and Mary Baker were more than a little concerned when they heard that Seth was dead, and received a summons to appear before the coroner's jury on the following morning. They tried, however, to put a bold face on the matter, and manifested no symptom of grief whatever.

In his examination John Baker made a revelation. Chips listened like one in a dream, scarcely believing his own ears.

"He was not the father of the children," he said. "In fact, he and his wife had never had any children. But they were his brother Robert's children. Chips had been named after his father, and had always been called Bob until the street boys of his acquaintance nicknamed him Chips, a name that had stuck to him. His brother Robert," he said, "was a good man, a kinder or honester had never lived; he was a very sober man, too, scarcely ever tasting drink; and his wife Jane was a good woman, and they loved each other dearly. They lived in a nice little house, and were very comfortable. One night, however, when Seth was about a year old, Robert's companions, who did not like his sober ways, made him drunk. It was said they drugged the beer: anyhow, he went home mad drunk. What happened nobody could tell exactly. But next morning he was found asleep on the floor, and his wife dead, with her head upon the fender, and a great gash in her temple. When Robert was awakened, he was horrified. He confessed all he knew about it, which was very little; he had a vague recollection of striking her with his fist—he had never spoken an unkind word to her before—but that was all. Well, he was found guilty of manslaughter, and sentenced to five years' penal servitude; but the knowledge that he had killed his wife, whom he loved so dearly, broke his heart; in less than a year he had pined himself to death. Well, as Mary and I had no children of our own, we took Robert's, and have brought them up as our own. They have earned a little sometimes by selling chips. On Christmas Eve they both went out as usual. Chips came home in the evening, but Seth never returned again. That's all I have to say, and all I know about the matter."

Chips knew that the latter part of this statement was false; but he was so astonished at what he had heard that he was unable to say anything.

Mary Baker corroborated all that her husband said, and there were no other witnesses to call. The medical evidence was that death had resulted from exposure to the very severe cold, and the jury returned a verdict in accordance therewith. And there the matter ended.

Before evening little Seth was locked up in a cheap parish coffin, and hidden for ever from human gaze. Chips remained sobbing on the floor till the last screw was driven in, then crept out of the room, and made his way with slow and listless steps to Bilkey's Court. That was the last night he ever spent there. When morning came he presented himself before his uncle and aunt with a strange hard look of determination upon his face.

" An' so you're not my father ? " he said, addressing his uncle.

" No, I'm not," said John Baker ; " but what of that?"

" On'y I'm glad of it," was the reply. " I'd rather my father were dead than be like you. I always told Seth I could 'member another home nor this; but you've killed him, but let me tell 'e you'll not kill me."

"You'd better not say that again, youngster," said his uncle fiercely, "or you'll rue it."

"It don't matter," was the reply; "you know 'tis true, an' it won't be very nice for 'e to 'member, I'm thinkin'."

"What won't be nice?" said John Baker savagely.

"Why, it won't be very nice, when the wind is a howlin' and the snow a-fallin', for 'e to think how you drove little Seth to death on sich a night."

For a moment John Baker seemed to quail before the stern gaze of the boy. Never in his life had Chips dared to answer him as he was doing.

"I'm not afear'd of 'e now," Chips went on, " so you needn't glower. An' you can't harm little Seth no more; you've done your worst by 'im. You drove 'im out when he were weak an' ill, an' not fit to be out o' his bed; think on it, an' he a little fatherless, motherless boy! I didn't say nothin' 'bout it at the inquest; but I'm thinkin' your memory 'll punish 'e enough afore you die. I'm off now. I'm fear'd I should get to hate you if I were to live 'ere now, an' I don't want to do that. So good-bye. I'm not your boy, an' I shall never come back 'ere no more." And before John Baker had time to reply, Chips was gone.

In Rusholme Road Cemetery they found room for all that was mortal of little Seth. Chips was the only mourner present at the funeral. He waited in the keen wind that swept with mournful sound across the graves till even the gravedigger had gone, then with a sigh turned away, and bent his steps towards the city, for he had yet to find a place of refuge where he might spend the night.

E

CHAPTER VIII.

NEW ACQUAINTANCES.

TO tell how, single-handed, Chips fought the world during the next two months would take too long. And, indeed, none but himself ever knew the sufferings and privations he endured; for the days, as a rule, were cheerless in the extreme, and the nights bitterly cold; and, worse than all, the sense of his loss and the utter loneliness of his life made his lot doubly hard to bear.

But there is one little circumstance we must mention before we pass on. On the Sunday morning after little Seth was buried, Chips was admitted again to a free breakfast in the school-room already mentioned at

Salford. It was with very listless steps that he made his way thither. He had spent the night underneath a stall in Shudehill Market, and had felt very lonely and sad : and when he crept out with the first glimmer of day, it was with a dull pain in his heart that was almost intolerable, and most sincerely did he wish that he might die too—that he might be freed from the burden of life. He was, however, quite in time for the breakfast, and crept in with the hungry crowd of children, and made his way to the seat he had once occupied with his brother ; for he had a vague feeling that somehow Seth would be nearer to him if he sat there. He had very great difficulty in keeping back the tears that started in his eyes continually; and when at length all the children stood up to sing grace, it was more than he could bear, and, hiding his face in his hands, he sobbed as though his heart would have broken.

By the time the buns and cocoa were handed round, he had recovered himself again, and devoured speedily enough the provisions that fell to his share. He felt in better spirits, too, after being warmed by the cocoa, and settled himself comfortably in a corner for the service that was to follow.

The children seemed thoroughly to enjoy the address, for the gentleman had evidently a large fund of anecdotes at his command, with which he illustrated and enforced the virtues of Honesty and Truthfulness and Kindness, and Sobriety and Industry and Perseverance ; closing his address by urging them to seek the help and friendship of the Saviour, who would never leave them nor forsake them.

Then he gave them the opportunity of asking questions on any matter that they would like more fully explained.

For several moments there was no response. And the gentleman opened his hymn-book for the purpose of announcing another hymn, when Chips suddenly sprang to his feet :

" If you please, sir," he said, " if it wouldn't be too much trouble like———." Then there was a sudden stop, for his voice had grown husky and his eyes full of tears.

" Don't be afraid, my lad," said the gentleman kindly " we are all friends here."

" 'Twern't that I was afraid," said Chips, pulling his sleeve across his eyes. " On'y my heart's been near broke lately, an' I thought, if 't'weren't too much trouble, I'd ax 'e to sing again, ' When Jesus comes.' "

" Oh yes, my lad, with pleasure," said the gentleman, " if you particularly wish it."

" The reason I axed," said Chips, " were because little Seth loved it so. You didn't know Seth, maybe ; but he were 'ere with me on'y last Sunday week. You must have seen him, I think. He was sich a bright little chap, was Seth, as full of fun as a guinea-pig, an' as happy as a cat in the sunshine. But he's gone now, sir ; I shall never 'ave my little Seth no more."

And Chips gulped down a great lump that had risen in his throat, and seemed for several seconds unable to say any more. Then he went on again :

" He went out to sell his chips on Christmas Eve, but he never comed back again. I watched an' waited for 'im all the night, but he never comed home. An all Christmas Day I searched for 'im, but I couldn't find 'im. Poor little chap ! he 'ad got tired, an' lay down in a gent's garden wi' his head upon his bundle ; an' the snow came down all the night an' covered 'im up ; an' in the mornin' he were smilin' as if he were very happy ; on'y his face was very white an' cold. But he didn't feel the cold, I reckon, for I guess he's in ' the better land.' "

And Chips began to sob again, many of the children keeping him company.

" I didn't mean to say all this," Chips went on after a while, in a tone of apology. " On'y the last time we was 'ere, Seth an' me, you sung, ' When Jesus comes ;' an' you don't know 'ow it comforted little Seth. He kept sayin' it over to hisself all the way 'ome, an' afore he dropped asleep that night I heard 'im sayin', soft like to hisself :

> " ' Oh, how His arms will rest me !
> When Jesus comes.'

An' the last time we was out together, an' his bundle was 'eavy an' the roads was very bad, he went away singin', his face as 'appy as anythink :

> " ' He'll know the way was dreary,
> When Jesus comes ;
> He'll know the feet grew weary,
> When Jesus comes.'

An' so I'd like for 'e to sing it again, sir, if it's not too much trouble, an' maybe it'll do me good ; an' I'd be mighty glad if Jesus 'ud come for me, for I'm terrible weary."

And Chips sat down with a jerk, and hid his face in his hands.

Then the gentleman got up, and spoke a few words of sympathy and encouragement to Chips, and ended by requesting that all the children would join him in singing the hymn that had been of so much comfort to the little boy that had so recently gone to " the better land."

Chips was not able to join in singing the hymn himself; yet it did him good, and he went away with a lighter heart than when be came.

Not far from the room he stumbled across a little cripple boy who was toiling wearily along on a pair of crutches.

" 'Ave you been to the breakfas' ? " said Chips.

" Aye," answered the little fellow, " I allers goes when I 'as the chance."

" Where do you live ? " said Chips.

" Long Mill Gate," was the reply.

" I used to live in Bilkey's Court, not far from there," said Chips.

" I know Bilkey's Court," said the boy.

" 'Ave you got any father ? " asked Chips.

" No ; but I've got a mother, and she's quite enough for me."

" What does she do ? "

" Gits drunk mostly."

" An' what do you do ? "

" Anything as turns up."

" What's your name ? " was Chips' next question.

" Joe Wigley."

" Shall I carry ye, Joe, for ye'll never get 'ome at this rate ? "

" Aye ; I'd be mighty 'bliged," said Joe, his eyes sparkling.

And the next minute Chips was bounding along the streets with the little cripple on his back. He scarcely felt his weight, while his heart felt all the lighter for doing this act of kindness.

In the days that followed, Chips often gave Joe a helping hand, for Chips was strong and active, and so was able to help the little cripple in many ways. And never did he stretch out his hand to help without feeling the better for it.

The gentleman who spoke to the children after their free breakfast never knew how much good his kindly words of counsel effected. In Chips they bore almost immediate fruit, and every day the lad tried to be honest and truthful and kind. If the gentleman had known, he would have been thankful indeed.

But Joe Wigley was not the only cripple whose acquaintance Chips made. There was yet another, who generally went by the name of " Old Ebenezer."

Ebenezer Wilks was about fifty years of age, but his hair and beard had gone quite white, which made him appear much older.

Ebenezer had been a cripple all his life, and for more than thirty years had spent his days in a little square waggon that ran on four six-inch wheels, which, by the aid of a couple of sticks, he was able to propel along the streets at a good rate. In this little waggon there was also room enough for a moderate-sized canister, in which Ebenezer kept his stock-in-trade, consisting chiefly of oranges, apples, toffee, and gingerbread nuts.

Ebenezer's toffee and gingerbread were always of the best kind—better could not be got in Manchester, and so in time he became noted for his honest dealings ; and as he always looked tidy and clean, his trade rapidly increased.

Since his mother died, ten years before, Ebenezer had lived by himself, and, as far as he knew, he had not a relative in the wide world.

He thought of this sadly sometimes, and wondered what he would do when he would be no longer able to help himself. It is true that he had saved a bit of money ; but if he were helpless, and had to trust the spending of it to the people around him, he knew that he would soon be penniless ; and many a night the old man lay awake thinking of these things, and in his heart sincerely hoped and prayed that he might be taken at once out of the world when he was no longer able to help himself.

Chips had known Ebenezer by sight, and had known his name ever since he could remember ; for at the time of which we write the old man was a well-known figure in many of the most busy thoroughfares of the city.

It was not, however, until more than two months after Seth's death that Chips and Ebenezer became acquainted ; and as that acquaintance formed an important epoch in Chip's history, we will tell, in the next chapter, how it came about.

CHAPTER IX.

"OLD EBENEZER."

IT was a dreary evening in March. All day there had been a continuous drizzle of rain, sufficient to keep the streets in a state of chronic puddle. Chips had been out since morning, and was in consequence drenched to the very skin, and was as miserable —as he afterwards expressed it—" as he could live an' hang together."

In order to avoid the crowd, he was making his way along a narrow and unfrequented street, wondering how he should while away the rest of the evening, and where he should spend the night.

His experience of lodging-houses such as he could afford to patronize had not been by any means happy. It was only by the rarest chance that he could get near the fire, and if he gave up his clothes to be dried, he ran the risk of never getting them back again. More than once his pockets had been picked while he slept, and in other ways he had been fleeced of his hard-earned coppers.

On the other hand, to creep under the market-stall in his wet clothes, and lie shivering all the night, was a prospect not by any means inviting. Moreover, it was Saturday night, and the market would be open till late, so that he would have to wait till midnight before he would be able to creep unobserved to his place of hiding.

There were no cocoa-rooms open then where he might spend an hour over a mug of "grateful and comforting." The only refuge seemed to be the public-house. And yet, since he heard that terrible story about his father, he almost shuddered at the name of drink.

What, then, was he to do? That was what he pondered over as he made his way slowly along the murky street in the fast-deepening twilight. A little way ahead of him he heard the rattle of the iron wheels of "Old Ebenezer's" little waggon, as the old man slowly propelled himself along; for Ebenezer seemed in a very sober mood this evening, and was evidently in no hurry to reach his lonely home.

"Poor old Ebenezer!" said Chips thoughtfully. "Maybe he's as wet an' miserable as me. I wonder where he lives, an' if he's anybody to look arter him?"

Then Chips' thoughts returned again to himself, and to the questions that had been troubling him before. A moment later he looked up as a drunken man reeled past him, muttering curses as he stumbled on.

"I'll never be a drunkard if I can help it," Chips said to himself. "Oh, dear! if it hadn't been for the drink, father an' mother an' little Seth might 'a been all livin', an' in that purty little 'ouse I sees in my dreams sometimes. Oh, dear! to think drink's done it all; an' 'ere I be without a 'ome, an' without a friend in the world."

What other reflections Chips might have indulged in it is impossible to say, had they not been rudely disturbed by a great noise and clatter that arose in the street a little ahead of him.

Running hastily forward, he soon discovered the cause of the clatter. Poor old Ebenezer was lying in the gutter apparently unconscious, his overturned waggon close to his side, while three or four yards ahead was the drunken man who had stumbled over him, slowly, and with many curses, struggling to his feet, and midway between the two was Ebenezer's canister, with all his stock-in-trade, fortunately none the worse. The drunkard, with brain soddened and senses steeped in alcohol, evidently did not know what he had stumbled over, for as soon as he regained his feet he went stumbling on as before, without casting a single glance behind him.

Ebenezer was only stunned, and—thanks to Chips' strong arms—he was soon seated in his little waggon, with his all but useless legs tucked underneath him, his canister under his nose, and his face once more turned towards home. But the poor old man seemed dazed and bewildered, and, seeing his distress, Chips —always ready to do a kindly deed—volunteered to help him home.

"Aye, boy, I'd be so glad," said the old man, " for I feel quite mazy like."

"All right," said Chips, fastening his bundle-strap to the old man's waggon. "Where to ?"

"Vixen Alley—off Ancoats. Do you know where it is ?"

"Oh, aye," he said; and off he started, carefully dragging the little waggon and its occupant behind him.

By the time they reached Vixen Alley, Ebenezer had pretty nearly recovered from the effects of his fall, but he insisted on Chips going in with him and sharing his supper.

Chips was surprised to see how nimbly—by the aid of a pair of crutches—the old man moved about the house. A lamp was lighted—as Chips afterwards declared—in no time, and a fire was soon crackling cheerily in the grate. Chips was quite surprised to find what a nice little house Ebenezer had. There were pictures on the papered walls, ornaments on the mantelpiece, cushions on the chairs, and even some strips of carpet on the floor.

"Now, get into that big chair and warm thyself," said Ebenezer, "for I see thou 'rt wet, and I daresay thou 'rt cold."

Chips thought he had never sat in such a comfortable seat before in his life, and while he dreamily

He nimbly hoisted himself on another chair on the other side

watched the faces in the fire, and conjured up all
kinds of pleasant pictures, Ebenezer busied himself in
getting supper ready. That done, he told Chips to
pull round his chair to the table, while he nimbly
hoisted himself on another chair on the other side.

Chips could scarcely believe his own eyes when he
looked around. Not only was there a white table-
cloth,—what he never remembered to have seen before
in his life,—but there were real china cups and
saucers, and a metal teapot, while among the eatables
were tinned beef, bread and butter, and even some
sweet biscuits.

Ebenezer did not eat much himself, but he helped
Chips largely, and watched him closely while he was
eating. Chips was by no means good-looking; but he
had an open, frank, pleasant face notwithstanding,
and Ebenezer was evidently much pleased with his
new acquaintance.

When Chips had finished eating, Ebenezer opened
a conversation, or, more correctly, began to ply his
guest with questions.

" You're a decent-looking lad, and I'm much obliged
to you for your kindness to me," he began; "and so
you'll excuse me if I ask you a few questions. In
the first place, where do you live?"

" Nowhere regular," said Chips, blushing. " Fact
is, I ain't got no home."

" Where are you're parents?"

" Dead."

" Any brothers or sisters?"

" Not now," said Chips huskily. " Seth died back
at Christmas, an' I'm all alone in the world now."

"Ah, that's sad," said the old man. "But what's your name?"

"Chips Baker.

"*Chips* Baker! What does 'Chips' stand for?"

"Well, my real name is Robert, or Bob, but everybody calls me Chips now."

"Where are you going to sleep to-night?"

"Don't know," said Chips. "I often sleeps under a stall in the market, but it'll be late to-night afore the coast is clear."

"You're in no hurry to get home, then?"

Chips smiled feebly as he answered, "Oh, no; I'm in no hurry to get '*ome*."

"Very good. Then perhaps you would not mind staying and helping me a bit? I've some toffee to make to-night, and I feel a bit mazy still, somehow."

"I'll be very glad to stay," said Chips, his face beaming with pleasure.

"Then stay, my lad," said the old man cheerily. "And now let's to work." And in a very short time Chips was initiated into the mysteries of toffee-making.

Chips never remembered an evening to slip away so quickly and pleasantly; and when at length he rose to go, he did so with a feeling of regret—almost of pain. He had his hand upon the door-latch before Ebenezer spoke:

"Look here, Chips—Bob, Robert—no, I'll call thee Robert,—I'm much obliged to thee; I am, indeed. And upon my conscience, I don't like sending thee adrift at this time of night, so if thou'lt stay for the night thou canst sleep on the sofa, and welcome."

Chips needed no second invitation. He made no reply, however. He felt that he dare not trust himself to speak, but he came back and sat down by the fire again; and far on into the night—long after Ebenezer was asleep in the room above—he sat there, wondering, at times, whether he was awake or dreaming.

The next day being Sunday, and a regular downpour of rain, the two remained in-doors, Ebenezer entertaining his guest by reading aloud from the New Testament. It was a new experience to the old man, and somehow, as the day wore away, he found his heart going out towards the orphaned homeless lad, whose broad homely face beamed upon him with pleasure and gratitude. Ebenezer had not spent such a pleasant Sunday since his mother died, and when he hoisted himself up the stairs that night on his crutches, after seeing Chips comfortable on the sofa, he felt as though he would like to have the lad with him always. There was such an honest expression on the lad's homely face, such a genuine ring in the tones of his voice, that it was a pleasure to have him about.

"Hi, Robert?" he said next morning, when Chips was about to start on his daily round; "you'd better come back here again this evening, lad, unless you find a better crib. I've nobody but myself, and there's plenty of room for us both; and if you like to come, you're welcome."

"I'm sure I'm much obliged," said Chips, the moisture gathering in his eyes. "An' I'd be very glad to come, on'y I don't like to put on your kindness in that way."

F

"Toot, toot, lad! say nothing about it. You've been kind to me, and one good turn deserves another Besides, you can help me a bit this evening, if you like to come."

"If I can help you, I'll be so thankful," said Chips feeling ready to cry. And away he went through the sloppy streets, with a lighter heart than he had known for many a month.

Stumbling over little Joe Wigley, as he was returning in the evening, he gave him a third of his profits as a kind of thank-offering; and little Joe, who had had but poor luck during the day, went on his way rejoicing. So three hearts were made happy that day, and *kindness* was the magic wand that did it all.

Chips found that he could help Ebenezer in many ways. And every evening there was always plenty to do. Not only had the toffee to be manufactured, but there was the house to clean, the victuals to cook, and their clothes to be washed and mended.

Old Ebenezer was quite clever at all these matters, and soon put Chips into the way of sweeping the house, dusting the furniture, and even washing the clothes.

So time wore on; and wet, windy, blustering March gave place to April's sunshine and showers. And still Chips remained with Ebenezer, nor thought of leaving him. In fact, they had become essential to each other. Ebenezer got to love Chips as though he had been his own son, and his cheerless, childless life became brighter than he ever hoped or dreamed. While Chips, who had never known a parent's love, regarded the old man in the light of a father, and confided to him all his history, and all his hopes and fears.

But when May came in at last, with long bright days and warm sunshine, and breezes warm and gentle, an old longing returned to Ebenezer, a longing that had been his with every returning May, but which had never yet been realized.

"I'll speak to the lad about it to-night," he said, as he squatted on his door-step enjoying the evening's sunshine. "Maybe we could manage it together, and if we could—Oh! if we could, I think I should desire no more."

CHAPTER X.

FERN COTTAGE.

"ROBERT," said Ebenezer that evening, as they sat over their supper in the deepening twilight, "I want to have a little talk with you, my lad, so we'll do no more to-night. It's the first of May to-day, and a glorious day it's been. I'm like a cat in one thing, Robert,—I love the sunshine. But every year for forty years, when May has come round, bright and warm and beautiful, I've had a great longing to go away into the country to live. Oh, I think if I could get away among the green fields and listen to the birds singing all the summer long, that I should live twenty years longer yet. I never spent but one whole day right away in the country in my life, Robert, and I think that was the happiest day I have ever known. But I was only a child then; and every year the town has got bigger, and pushed the country farther and farther away. And for years now my poor old heart has been aching for a sight of the country,—real country, I mean,—but aching in vain."

" Never mind," said Chips cheerfully, " I'll take 'e away right beyond Cheetham Hill some day. There's country there—fields and trees, an' all."

" Wait a minute, Robert," said Ebenezer. " I'm talking about living in the country altogether. In the winter, the city and noise, and my little home here in this narrow court, are bearable; but oh ! in the summer I want to see the streams flashing in the sunshine, and hear the music of the wind in the trees, and listen to the singing of the birds, and watch the contented cattle in the fields. O Robert, Robert ! I've read about it in books, and heard my mother talk about her home in the country, until my heart has nearly burst with longing."

" It 'ud be very nice, I guess," said Chips, " but I never hope for owt so fine."

" I grew flowers in a long box on the window-sill once," went on Ebenezer, without heeding Chips' remark, " but the court got so smoky at last that they all died; and I think sometimes that I'll die too, if I stay here much longer. But if I had a little house in the country, with room to grow flowers, and vegetables, and trees, around where the birds could sing, then I'd be happy. I've been studying gard'ners' books for years, and I know the proper times for sowing seeds, and the proper seeds to sow; and sometimes in dreams I've fancied myself in my little waggon, or hopping round on my crutches, weeding the beds and watering the flowers. O Robert, Robert! will my dreams ever come true?"

"Dunno, I'm sure," said Chips, looking puzzled. "All you say 'ud be glorious, but the livin's to be got somehow, and there 'ud be nobody in the country to buy chips or toffee; so I can't see as 'twould work."

"But if we had a large garden where we could grow vegetables, and fruits, and flowers; and you could come into market twice a week to sell them? Think of that, Robert; wouldn't you look fine driving a nice pony and cart, like a young gent?" And the old man rubbed his hands with glee.

"But all that would cost money," said Chips, shaking his head; "an' I know nowt 'bout gardenin'."

'But I've got some money, Robert," Ebenezer went on. "I've done a good business for thirty years now, an' I've put away a few pounds every year. I do think we could manage; we could employ a practical gardener to do the chief part of the work. I could weed the beds and 'tend to the flowers, and you could help the gardener and come to market. Now, listen to this, my lad, and say what you think of it."

And Ebenezer read from that day's newspaper an advertisement of a cottage to be let, with a large garden attached, and situated about eight miles from Manchester and two miles from Buckley Railway Station.

"Well," said Chips, scratching his head, "I'd like it 'mazingly, but I'm fear'd it's too good to hope for."

" Anyhow, Robert, we'll have a holiday to-morrow, and go and look at it. We can get to London Road Station for the eight o'clock train, and you'll be able to lift me in and out of the carriage like anything; and won't I get over the ground from Buckley, that's all, lor' bless us ! I feel fair young again at the thoughts of it."

Far on into the night Ebenezer and Chips chatted about the cottage and the garden and the joys of country life; and when they went to bed it was still to think and dream of country lanes and green fields, and rippling streams and singing birds.

The next morning dawned clear and glorious. Ebenezer and Chips were at the station half an hour before the train started, and when they got fairly under way, their excitement knew no bounds. A journey by rail was a new experience in the lives of both of them. Oh, what joy it was to leave the noisy, smoky city behind them, and to drink in the pure country air, fragrant with the breath of ten thousand flowers !

The country children looked curiously at them as they passed them on the road from Buckley Station, but to be stared at was nothing new in the experience of Chips and Ebenezer.

They reached the cottage at length,—Fern Cottage it was called,—and both fell in love with it at first sight; it seemed to them a veritable Paradise, a perfect little bower of beauty. We readily grant that neither of them could be considered fastidious ! a thatched cottage on a lonely moor would have been a joy and delight to both. And yet few people would have denied that Fern Cottage was a pretty spot.

It stood at the foot of a wooded slope known as ' the plantation," and faced due south. On the east it was bounded by two close lines of poplars, and, behind these, two other lines of sombre-looking pines. These trees had been planted by the late owner and occupier — a maiden lady, six months deceased — for the purpose of screening the cottage from the east winds. To the west, and in front, was a large garden, divided by a gravel path leading down from the front door to a stream of clear water, that rippled pleasantly over its stony bed all day long.

Both cottage and garden had been well kept, for the old lady had taken great pride in both, and sufficient time had not yet elapsed since her death for many marks of decay to be visible. Moreover, John Pearson, who lived with his wife and only child Jane, in a cottage near, had still given an eye to the place, for in the late occupier's time he had been gardener, groom, and general *factotum.*

Since her death John had been compelled to stick to his last, for he was a shoemaker by trade, yet he was not without hope that when Fern Cottage got a new tenant he might be employed as of old.

The cottage might have been let twenty times over had it not been so far from the station. That seemed the one great drawback in the eyes of all who had come to look at it, though the agent saw other difficulties in the way of its being well let. The cottage was too large for any of the working class in the neighbourhood ; it was too small for people who could afford to live in the country and keep a carriage ; and it was too far from the station for business men, who

would have to go and return from the city every day
So for six months it had remained empty, and seemed
likely to remain so for many months more.

John Pearson was very civil to Ebenezer and Chips
and readily showed them all over the place, though
he much wondered what two such comical-looking
individuals could want with a place like Fern Cottage.
But he had heard such wonderful stories before now
about great people in disguise and rich people looking
like paupers, that he had come to the conclusion, before
he had answered half of Ebenezer's questions, " that
very likely the old man was as rich as a Jew."

So John was very civil and pleasant spoken, and
asked them if they would honour him by coming into
his cottage and having a cup of tea with their dinner,
an invitation which was gratefully accepted.

Then Chips and Ebenezer took a ramble in the
plantation, and it was wonderful to see how nimbly
the old man hopped from place to place on his
crutches, and a pleasure to watch his beaming face.
Both he and Chips were very silent, for their hearts
were too full for speech. Forty years had passed
away since Ebenezer had spent a day in the country.
And, oh, what a long stretch of wilderness those
years seemed to him, as he lay there under the
whispering trees, with his thoughts far back in the
past ! What a weary round of toil from day to day !
What hopeless misery and pain ! And now Chips
had come to him, or perhaps had been sent of God,
and with his help there was a hope at last that the
long dream of his life might be realized ; and as the
old man thought of these things, silent tears rolled

down his bronzed and withered cheeks, the first he had shed for years. He almost wondered if he were not dreaming—if those pleasant dreamy sounds of wind and stream were not the imaginings of his weary spirit longing to be free.

Chips had left Ebenezer to his meditations, and had gone off on an exploring expedition on his own account. Reaching the top of the hill behind the house, from which an extensive view of surrounding country was to be obtained, he felt as though he would like to shriek for very joy and delight. And very likely he would have done so had he not espied, in a sunny hollow of the hill not far below him, little Jane Pearson,—or Jenny, as she was always called,—searching for primroses.

A sweet shy child was Jenny, with soft blue eyes, and a wealth of flaxen hair. She made Chips think of what he had heard about the angels. He thought he had never seen so pretty a child in all his life. He was strongly tempted to go down and help her search for flowers, but his bashfulness prevented him; and so he contented himself with watching her through half-closed eyes as she moved about among the ferns, all unconscious of his presence.

He did not know then that she was John Pearson's child, for she had kept herself out of sight while he and Ebenezer were in the house.

What a pleasant dreamy day that was! what an oasis in the desert of their lives! and yet, when evening came, it seemed to bring with it a sense as of something lost—of a joy that had come and gone, leaving only a memory and a regret.

Ebenezer did not sleep a wink that night, though he retired to rest early, for he was sorely perplexed as to what he should do for the best. To rent the cottage and garden—and he would need an adjoining field or two as well—would be an important undertaking. He might lose all the money that he had worked so hard to get, and striven so long to save. On the other hand, it might prove a great success, and by investing his little capital in this way he might be able to live in comfort for the rest of his days.

Moreover, after this glimpse of the country, he felt as though he could never endure the dirty noisy town again. He felt as though he had not room to breathe; and if now he gave up this dream of his life, he thought he would break his heart and die. So by morning he had settled the question for ever. And before the bright sunny month was at an end, Ebenezer and Chips had taken up their abode at Fern Cottage, and John Pearson had been installed as gardener-in-chief.

CHAPTER XI.

A FRIEND IN NEED.

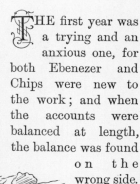

THE first year was a trying and an anxious one, for both Ebenezer and Chips were new to the work; and when the accounts were balanced at length, the balance was found on the wrong side. Still the old man was not discouraged. He knew that the year had been an unusually expensive one. He had spent a good deal in fruit-trees and in seeds and manure—

more than would be necessary for him to spend again; and so he started the second year in faith and hope, and realized at the end of the year all he had hoped for.

He and Chips were fairly on their legs now, and two happier mortals there were not on earth. They had reached the loftiest height of their ambition, had compassed all their desire, and so were content.

Twice a week Chips drove to market with his garden produce. And now he began to reap some little fruit from the hard and stony ground of his early experience. His customers soon discovered that they had no country bumpkin to deal with in Chips. He was quick, sharp-witted, and never lost an opportunity. But they discovered another thing: they discovered that he was strictly honest and truthful, and that if he recommended an article they might rely upon its being good. In the old days of weariness and want, he had proved by experience that honesty was the best policy; but now, under Ebenezer's tuition, he had got to love honesty for its own sake, and was gradually growing toward a Christian life.

Chips never went into town without taking with him something for his little cripple friend, Joe Wigley, and Joe was always on the watch for his coming. The little fellow did not grow very much, and it was very clear that he would never be anything but a cripple all the days of his life. It was a sad destiny, though he never complained, and, if he could get food from day to day, seemed quite content.

So three years had passed away since Chips commenced to tread his new path of life, when one Tuesday he missed Joe from his accustomed place: he did not trouble about this at first, thinking he would turn up some time during the day. But though Chips waited about some time after he had disposed of all his goods, Joe did not put in an appearance. And Chips had to return to Fern Cottage without a sight of his little friend. He did not, however, make himself very uneasy about the matter, thinking that something must have turned up unexpectedly, and that he would be at the old place on Saturday morning.

But on Saturday morning Chips was disappointed again. Joe was not at the old spot, and Chips could not help fearing that something had happened to the little fellow—that he was sick, or had been run over, or perhaps killed.

"I must get to know what's up," he said to himself, striding rapidly in the direction of Long Mill Gate, having finished his business in the market. "If the little chap's in trouble, I must help him if I can. But how to find him's the difficulty."

It was a warm afternoon in June, with a soft gentle breeze in the country that was delightfully refreshing; but in Long Mill Gate, and in the courts and alleys leading therefrom, the air was stagnant and laden with the foulest smells. Chips felt as though he would be smothered, and wondered how, in the old life, he could have existed in such an atmosphere.

Going up to a group of ragged, sickly-looking urchins, who were playing pitch-and-toss with half-pennies, he inquired if any of them knew a little lad that walked on crutches, called Joe Wigley.

"I knows 'im," shouted one of the lads; "but 'e lives in Hangel Meadow, I'm thinkin'."

" Then you're thinking wrong," said Chips.   " He lives hereabouts somewhere."

" Been down i' the pecker lately ? " queried another of the lads.

" Very likely," said Chipps.

' Mother got mar'red again an' cleared out ? " asked the same lad.

" I know nothing about that," said Chips.

" Lives in top 'ouse, 13 Court, top room, unless ow'd woman's turned him out."

" Thanks," said Chips, and started at once to find No. 13 Court.

This was easily done.   It was a foul place.   The whole court was reeking with all manner of uncleanness.   At the top house an old woman was squatted in the open doorway, smoking a short pipe.

" If you please," said Chips, addressing her, " does Joe Wigley live here ? "

" Aye," she snarled.   " I wish he didn't."

" Is he well ? "

" Aye, well enoo, only he won't own to it.   But I'll bundle 'im out afore he's many days older, unless he looks arter gettin' the rent."

" Is he much in debt ? " asked Chips.

" Aye, goin' on a fortnight, an' his mother's cleared out for good an' all."

" What a shame ! " said Chips.

" Don't know," growled the old woman ; " he's better without her."

" Can I see him ? " was Chips' next question.

" Aye, if thou likes ; he's in the garret."

Up the rickety, rotting stairs Chips bounded, and

into the stifling garret. For a moment he could scarcely see anything, it was so dark.

"Who's there?" called a feeble voice from the darkest corner of the room.

"Why, Joe, what's the matter?" said Chips, going towards what seemed only a dirty bundle of rags.

Slowly the little fellow raised himself to a sitting posture. "Well, this is good of you, Chips," he said, smiling feebly.

"Why, what is the matter with you?" said Chips, kneeling by his side.

"Dunno, Chips; on'y I feel clean done beat."

"Sorry for that," said Chips, producing a dozen large ripe strawberries that he had gathered purposely for Joe that morning. "Come, eat these, my lad, and you'll feel better, I'll wager."

"You are good," said Joe, smiling again; but though he tried his best, he could not eat all the strawberries. "I'll keep 'em 'gin to-morrow," he said, lying down again on the dirty rags.

"This will never do," said Chips; "you'll never get better at this rate."

"Don't much matter, I'm thinkin'," was the quiet answer.

"Oh, nonsense, Joe; don't talk in that way; never say die, my lad; keep your heart up, and you'll be well again in no time."

"Guess not, Chips; I'm clean done."

"Not a bit of it," said Chips cheerfully, though he saw that Joe was very ill, dying for lack of fresh air and wholesome food. "I'll make it all right about the rent, and send up something nice for you to eat;

and when I come into town on Tuesday, I'll call again."

"I reckon I shan't be 'ere by then," Joe answered.

"Not here? Then where will you be?" said Chips with a laugh, though he felt more ready to cry.

"Nowhere."

Chips turned back again, and looked at him. "Are you in any pain?" he asked.

"No, Chips; never 'ad no pain."

"Hungry?"

"Not now: I was at first."

Chips turned away again, and walked toward the door. What should he do? He did not think Joe had any disease; he was simply exhausted, and if left alone much longer, he would die. What should he do? The old question came back again. Suppose it was little Seth who lay there, instead of Joe Wigley, what would he do then? That question decided the matter.

"Joe," he said, going up to the bedside, "if I were to bring the pony and trap round here, would you go home with me? I mean, do you think you are strong enough?"

Instantly the little fellow's eyes brightened. "Oh, aye," he said, sitting up in bed again, "I could manage that, I'm sartin."

"Eat up the strawberries, then, and this piece of cake, if you can manage it, and I'll be back for you in half an hour."

Chips wondered what Ebenezer would say. Still he felt that he could not do other than he was doing.

All the court turned out to see Joe off. The little

fellow looked very wan and thin, but his eyes were bright, and there was a hopeful smile upon his face.

During the first part of the journey he reclined in a corner of the trap quite still, with eyes half closed, and apparently taking no notice of anything. But when at length the noisy streets gave place to the quiet country lanes, and the wilderness of bricks and mortar disappeared, and instead broad vistas of country, clad in summer's beauty, stretched away until they touched the distant sky, Joe's eyes instantly brightened, and his face became radiant with delight.

" Oh, Chips ! " he exclaimed, " are this the country ? "

" Aye," said Chips ; " have you never seen it before ? "

" Never," was the laconic reply.

" Pretty, ain't it ? " said Chips, pleased to see his little friend so animated and interested.

" It's glorious," said Joe, gazing round him with wide-open eyes, and a glow of pleasure mantling his wan cheeks. Then he became quiet again, but not indifferent to what was passing around him. Now and then he asked Chips to stop the pony for a moment, that he might hear the birds singing in the trees, and after listening for awhile, he would nod his head, and Chips would drive on again.

It was a glorious evening. There was just breeze enough to bend the sedgy grass by the waysides and stir the foliage on the trees ; across the fields the hedges flung long shadows, and the slanting sunbeams fringed every moving leaf and blade with amber and gold. In the west the sky glowed like a furnace, and the few clouds that hung lightly in the heavens took all hues and shapes——now vanishing almost from sight, and now glowing as if washed in gold.

" Fine, ain't it ? " said Chips, after he had driven on a long time in silence.

" I ain't got no word as means it," said Joe, drawing a long breath, and for the rest of the way he kept silence.

He was quite exhausted by the time they reached Fern Cottage, and for some time had lain on a heap of straw in the bottom of the trap.

Ebenezer was getting quite anxious about Chips, he was so late ; but when he heard the noise of wheels, he hopped to the gate on his crutches to meet him.

" Hi, Robert," he said, " thou'rt very late, my lad ; what's amiss ? "

" I've been to see a friend," said Chips, " and brought him home with me."

" A friend ? " questioned Ebenezer. " I don't see anybody."

" Here he is," said Chips, lifting out Joe in his arms, and running with him into the house. Up the stairs he bounded, and laid Joe in his own bed, and then fetched a glass of milk, which the little fellow drank eagerly.

" I couldn't help it, uncle," he said, turning to the old man at length. " I found him all alone, dying for want of fresh air and food. He'll get better here, I'm certain ; and I couldn't leave him alone to die."

" You did quite right, Robert," said the old man with evident emotion. " And I'm glad you've got such a kind heart. Nobody ever lost anything by being kind, Robert; and you'll get your reward for this, my lad."

For two or three days Joe's life seemed to tremble in the balance; then he began to rally, and in a little while he was able to get out into the sunshine, and to climb the hill behind the house. And long before the summer was over he was able to assist Ebenezer in weeding the beds and gathering in the fruit. So time went on, and Joe got quite strong at length. It is true he will always be lame, but he manages now with only one crutch, and sometimes he walks short distances with only a stick. To Chips he fills the place, to some extent, once occupied by little Seth, and neither Chips nor Ebenezer will ever hear of him leaving the cottage.

CHAPTER XII.

CONCLUSION.

CHIPS has nearly lost his old familiar nickname now. Ebenezer always calls him Robert, Joe and Jenny Pearson call him Bob, while John Pearson and his wife speak of him as Master Robert, or the young master.

The garden has been greatly enlarged since they went to live at Fern Cottage, and is now at least double the size it was formerly; and still they keep extending their borders while their business steadily increases.

A housekeeper presides over the domestic arrangements of the cottage now, assisted by Jenny Pearson, who runs in every day; and to at least one of the family she seems like a gleam of sunshine, and he is never so happy as when she is about. Chips has lost all his bashfulness, and Jenny is not nearly so shy as she used to be. Sometimes they may be seen in the plantation together gathering wild flowers, or sitting side by side on a mossy bank, engaged in very animated conversation.

Chips has grown to be quite a good-looking young fellow, while in mind and manners he has improved quite as much as in appearance. During the first three winters of his residence at the cottage, he spent four evenings every week at a night school in the village of Buckley, while he did a large amount of miscellaneous reading at home.

" It was not until he began to know something," he says, " that he discovered he knew nothing at all." And having found out that he had a mind, he set to work to improve it with all possible haste.

Chips is no genius or paragon of excellence; but he is an honest, truthful, industrious, persevering young Englishman, and, in these degenerate days, that is saying a great deal. His face is browned by wind and sun, and his hands are hard with ceaseless toil; but his heart is tender and his conscience clear. He makes no parade of his goodness, but he tries to do his duty in the sight of God and man.

He has never forgotten the simple little sermon on " A good name is rather to be chosen than great riches;" and daily he tries to act out the teachings of the New Testament, and to trust in that Saviour who lived and died for all. He is not a member of the Royal Exchange yet, though he has stood upon its floor, and read the Scripture around its dome.

He has never seen his uncle and aunt since that memorable morning — well, no matter how many years ago. Months after, when time had soothed his sorrow, and the hard feeling he had cherished in his heart towards them had passed away, he paid a visit to Bilkey's Court, but the old home was inhabited by strangers. John and Mary Baker had gone away, but no one knew whither. He has made inquiries many times since, but without avail.

Old Ebenezer bids fair to live twenty years longer yet. He says, since he came to Fern Cottage, that he has renewed his youth, like the eagle. He has never visited Manchester since he left, nor has he any desire to do so. A few people were rather surprised at the old man's sudden disappearance, and instituted a few inquiries respecting him; but the multitude did not give the matter a second thought. It was reported at length that the old man was dead, and as there was nobody to contradict it, it was generally believed. Months after, when the old man heard of it, he rubbed his hands gleefully. "Dead, eh?" he exclaimed; "why, bless us, I'm only beginning to live!"

It would be difficult to find three happier people than Ebenezer, Chips, and Joe. During the bright summer days they spend all their time out of doors, going into the house only to eat and sleep. On summer evenings they may be seen reclining on a mossy bank at the end of the cottage, enjoying the quiet beauty of the dying day. In the plantation they hear the birds singing their evening hymn of praise, while the brook rippling through the garden chants a pleasant accompaniment, and the evening breeze swells the song.

One by one the pale stars of God come out to deck the brow of night. The birds hush their songs and fold their wings to rest, but the wind still makes dreamy music in the plantation, and the brook ripples on as before.

At length the old man reaches out his hand for his crutches, murmuring to himself, but loud enough for the others to hear, " When I consider the heavens, the work of Thy fingers, the moon and the stars which Thou hast ordained, what is man that Thou art mindful of him, or the son of man that Thou visitest him ? " Then, after a moment's pause, he murmurs again, " Surely God is good."

" Aye, uncle, that He is," say Chips and Joe in chorus.

" Then let us thank Him, lads, and go to rest."

OUR JOE.

CHAPTER I.

LEFT ALONE.

"The way seems dark about me—overhead
The clouds have long since met in gloomy spread,
And when I looked to see the day break through,
Cloud after cloud came up with volume new."

"THOU'LT not mind bein' left alone for once, Joe?"

"Nay, mother," was the cheerful answer; "I'll be all right, never fear.

"I'm main sorry to leave thee, lad," she went on; "but thy father's none so well, as thou knows."

"Aye, he's a bit out o' the square, I know," Joe answered.

"I tell thee I am fair frightened sometimes," the

mother answered; "those fainting do's come on so sudden."

"But he'll be all right again in a bit, I 'spects', ' Joe replied; "so I wouldn't worrit, if I were you, mother."

"I can't help worriting, Joe, try as I will," was the reply. "I've so many things to vex me an' make me anxious. Thou knows we've had no luck lately."

"Aye, I know; but p'r'aps you'll have good luck to-day."

"I hope so," was the somewhat dubious reply. "If we don't, I'm sure I don't know what's to become of us. Thou knows we shall need coals to-night, and the rent is over-due already."

"Aye, but we've always rubbed along some road," said Joe thoughtfully; then added, after a moment's pause, "I wish I were able to go out with you."

"But thou mustn't think of walkin' wi' that bad foot of thine," the mother replied quickly. "It'll never get well without restin'."

"If I'd gone barefoot, instead of wearin' them 'bominable owd boots," Joe answered, "I'd been as right as ninepence."

"Aye, likely 'nough," was the answer; "but thou knows it may be all for the best, so thou must be patient."

"Well done, mother," said Joe, with a laugh, at the same time throwing his arms round her neck and kissing her; I *do* like to hear yer talk in that way—it sounds downright good an' cheerful."

"Does it, Joe?" the mother answered, with a

feeble smile. " Anyhow, I like to see thee laugh, my lad, and hear thee as weel. But there, thy father's callin', so I must be off. Good mornin', an' keep thy heart up." And shouldering a bundle of split canes, she lifted the door-latch, and stepped out into the dismal court.

" You'll be home as early as you can, mother ? ' Joe called after her.

' Aye, lad, never fear that," was the answer, and the next minute she was gone.

For a while Joe stood staring vacantly at the closed door, then muttered to himself, " I do wish that things were different—that's a fact ; " and with a little sigh he turned round and hobbled towards the fire-place, and commenced raking together very carefully the few lumps of coal that were smouldering in the grate. That being accomplished, he sat himself down on a rickety three-legged stool, with his elbows on his knees and his face on his hands, and gave himself up to reflection.

It was a dismal room in which he found himself. A very old bedstead in one corner, a round table in the centre much the worse for wear, two chairs, and a three-legged stool, with a few pots and pans, completed the furniture. But Joe had never been used to luxuries in the shape of furniture, and under ordinary circumstances would scarcely have given either room or furniture a second thought.

But to-day, to use his own words, " he was all down in the mouth." It was a new experience to him to be confined in-doors while his parents went out without him, and more than once he felt his anger kindle against the woman who, in all kindness, had given him the shoes that had caused the festering wound in his heel.

Indeed, so angry did he feel at length that he caught up the offending shoes and flung them on the fire, then watched them slowly smoulder with something like a smile of satisfaction lighting up his homely face.

" Anyhow, they'll help out the fuel a bit," he said to himself, rubbing his hands together ; and with this reflection he resumed his old position, and gave himself up to thought once more.

Now and then he raised his head and glanced through the grimy window, but only for a moment. Joe always disliked winter, and in his heart he was longing for summer-time to come again.

Since he could remember, he had led, with his parents, the life of a gipsy : keeping in the country while the summer lasted, and sleeping at nights in a little tent they always carried round with them. But when winter came, with its cold days and long dreary nights, they betook themselves to some large town or city, and hired a room for the winter. In this way Joe had become acquainted with most of the large towns in the country, as well as with its remote villages. Still, he could not " abide " the towns, and always hailed the first approach of spring with almost rapturous delight.

But in all his experience he could never remember beginning a winter so badly as this ; and as he crouched over the cheerless fire of smouldering coals and shoe leather, he could not help asking himself the question that he had often asked before, but never with any satisfactory result, viz., "Why his parents chose the life they did ? "

He had seen enough of life in town and country to satisfy him that no life could be more cheerless or comfortless than that of a travelling tinker. Then why had his father chosen it ? He knew that years ago, long before he was born, his father had been a journeyman blacksmith, nor was he unskilful at his trade ; while his mother had lived with her parents in a quiet Lancashire village before she was married, and had been very happy there, far happier than she had ever been since, if he might judge from hints that fell from her lips every now and then. It seemed strange, therefore, that they should have adopted their present mode of living.

Now and then he had questioned them relative to the matter, but had never received any satisfactory reply, and he had tried not to trouble himself any further about it.

But, somehow, to-day the old question haunted him again, and a vague feeling of unrest and dissatisfaction took possession of him.

He thought of the happy cottage homes he had seen in his wanderings up and down the country, and of the bonny, bright-faced children that played on the door-step or romped in the garden. He had seen cheerful fires burning in polished grates, and soft mats and carpets on the floor. He had seen tables with white cloths on them, and shining cups and saucers on gilded trays. He had peeped through cottage windows sometimes, and seen boys and girls busy with books

and toys ; and sometimes he had caught the strains of
some little hymn they were singing, and had wondered
how they learnt such pretty tunes, and where.   But
all these things had seemed far away from him—
something beyond the reach of his brightest dreams.

Yet, to-day, as he crouched, cold, comfortless, and
in pain, he felt as though things were not as they
ought to be.   Why could not his parents provide a
bright happy home as well as other people ?   He
knew that his father earned "lots " of money sometimes, but somehow he never did any good with it.
" Those streaks of good luck," as his father called
them, nearly always ended in a drunken bout, and left
them worse off than they were before.   Of course, his
father had a right to spend his money as he pleased ;
at least, he had always thought so.

But suppose he had thought wrongly about that
matter : suppose his father had a higher duty than
spending his money simply on his own pleasure ?
Somehow, to-day, things began to appear in a different
light to what they had ever done before, and the old
content was leaving him altogether.

Was it the cheerless day, or the cheerless room, or
the pain, or the cold, or was it through being left
alone, that he felt so dissatisfied ?

Perhaps all these things contributed to his dissatisfaction.   At any rate he sprang to his feet at length
with clenched fists and a look of determination upon
his face, as though about to fight some invisible foe.

" Look here, Joe Bradley," he said, half aloud,
" you'll be a man some day if you live long enough,
and you needn't be a travelling tinker unless you

like, an' you know you don't like it. So keep your weather-eye open, and who knows what'll turn up ?"

Joe seemed in a somewhat better frame of mind after the delivery of this soliloquy, and proceeded forthwith to mend the fire, though with a very sparing hand, for coals were scarce, and he knew it would "take him all his time," as he expressed it, to make them last the day out.

Soon after noon he cooked the herring his mother had left him, and ate the last morsel of bread in the house. Fortunately the herring and bread were sufficient to satisfy his hunger, and, comforted and somewhat warmed by the repast, he threw himself on the bed, and soon forgot all his troubles and discontent in a deep and dreamless sleep.

CHAPTER II.

IN THE NIGHT.

"Her cabined, ample spirit,
  It fluttered and failed for breath;
To-night it doth inherit
  The vasty hall of death."
                —MATTHEW ARNOLD.

WHEN Joe awoke it was quite dark. Moreover, the fire was out, and, what was worse still, he had no means of rekindling it, or even of obtaining a light. He did not trouble himself much, however.

"Mother an' the dad will soon be home now," he said to himself; "an' then we'll have a fire again in no time."

So he wrapped himself up in some old shawls on which he had been lying, for he felt terribly cold, and then lay down again to listen for the footfalls of his parents.

Every now and then he started up with the exclamation on his lips, " There they be at last ! " But the footfalls always passed his door, or else ceased ere they reached it.

" I wonder what can have kept 'em," he said to himself at length. " I'm sure it must be gettin' late. I wish there was a clock about as I could hear strike, for I'm all at sea 'bout the time o' day."

And indeed the hour was much later than he had any suspicion of. Still, Joe was not one of the timid sort, nor was he in the habit of going half-way to meet trouble. So he tried to make the best of the situation, and waited with as much patience as he could command.

But as the minutes grew into hours, and the hours dragged their slow length along, the silence became horribly oppressive. Almost imperceptibly the far-off roar of the city had died away into silence, and the tramp of feet had grown less and less, until it had ceased altogether. It seemed quite an age since the last echo of a policeman's measured tread had died away in the distance. And now everything was as still as the grave. All around him the great city slept, and not even the ticking of a clock or the purring of a cat kept him company in his silent and lonely vigil. Again and again he tried to sleep, but the more he tried the wider awake he seemed to get. Moreover, as the night wore slowly away, a sense as of coming trouble began to oppress him. He felt certain that something must have happened either to his father or mother, or they would have been at home long ere this. He knew how anxious his mother was about his foot, and he remembered, too, that her last words to him were that she would be home early.

Still he was quite disposed to hope for the best. Perhaps they would turn up first thing in the morning, and he might discover then that it was some very simple circumstance that had kept them.

So he battled with his fears and misgivings hour after hour, till, worn out with watching and anxiety, he dropped off again into a troubled sleep. How long the sleep lasted he never knew. But he started up at length in a state of terror, and stared eagerly round the room.

" I'm sure I heard a cry o' some sort," he said to himself. " Aye, an' there it is again."

" Mother! oh, mother!" like the cry of a terror-stricken child, fell distinctly on his ears.

In a moment he was out of bed, regardless of his bad foot, and, pulling open the door, he stood for a moment on the doorstep and listened. The night was perfectly still. Not even a passing footfall broke the silence, while the dense fog still hung like a pall over the city, blotting out every street light, and filling " Angel's Court" with Egyptian darkness.

Yet just across the way a feeble light was doing its best to struggle through the window, and from out that window came a child's sad wail again, " Oh, mother! mother!"

He listened intently, but no answer came to the child's appeal.

Then a piercing shriek, not loud or long, rang out in the darkness, but it was still the voice of the child.

Joe did not hesitate any longer now, but hopped across the street with all possible haste, and reached the door just as it was being thrown open, and so found himself suddenly face to face with a little girl of some nine or ten years of age. Joe was the first to recover himself, for the child seemed too utterly astonished to speak.

"What is the matter with you, little girl?" Joe said, as kindly as he knew how.

But all the answer he got was a terrified stare.

"Was it you as was a-callin' 'mother' just now?" Joe continued, in sympathetic tones for he saw that the child was too terrified to speak.

The word "mother," however, seemed to bring her to herself, for she answered quickly:

"Oh, yes, mother's terrible bad, an' won't speak. Be you a doctor?"

"Oh, no, I don't think so," Joe answered. "My name's Joe Bradley, and I live t'other side o' the court."

"An' you are not a bad man, or a robber?" she asked, eyeing him suspiciously.

"I ain't no man at all," said Joe, with a laugh. "I'm only a big, clumsy lump of a boy."

"Then I wish you'd come in an' try an' wake mother," was the tearful reply, "for I never seen her so white afore in my life."

So, without another word, Joe followed the child into the room, and up to the side of the bed.

He had never seen death before, but one glance was

sufficient to tell him what had happened, and with a low cry he started back and dropped into a chair.

"Why do you look that way?" the child asked; "why don't you speak to mother?"

"It's no use," said Joe, in a husky voice; "she couldn't hear if I was to speak."

"Why couldn't she hear?" asked the terrified child; "she always come'd round other times after a bit."

"But she won't come round this time," said Joe solemnly.

"Not never no more?" she asked, with a frightened look in her eyes.

Joe nodded his head in reply.

"Oh, you are a story-teller!" she cried fiercely; and again rushed up to the bed, calling, "Mother! mother!"

"Please don't," said Joe; "for don't you see she ain't livin'?"

"Ain't livin'!" she repeated after him, as if quite unable to comprehend his words.

"No, she ain't livin'," said Joe seriously; "she won't never live no more."

"Is she gone away to heaven?" the child asked.

"Aye," Joe answered quickly, glad of any form of words that would enable the child to comprehend that her mother was dead.

At that she dropped on the floor and burst into tears, and Joe glided stealthily up to the bed and pulled the white sheet over the dead face, then returned again to her, and began stroking her soft hair with his brown hand. He never had a sister of his own ; moreover, this little girl was in trouble, and so his heart went out to her instinctively, and he longed to help and comfort her all he could.

For a long time she sat at his feet sobbing quietly, and Joe kept wondering what he ought to do in a case like this. Ought he to go out and rouse the neighbours, and tell them what had happened, or should he wait till morning ?

At length the girl looked up, and, smiling through her tears, said brokenly, " Mother's 'appy now; for heaven's a beautiful place, ain't it ? "

" Well, as to that, I can't say," said Joe thoughtfully, " for I don't remember as ever I've been there."

" Of course you ain't been there," was the answer ; " folks don't go there till they dies."

" Oh, indeed ! " said Joe, somewhat taken aback ; " I never seen anybody as wasn't alive afore."

" But ain't you heard 'bout heaven ? " his companion asked.

" Oh, aye ! " he replied, " I've heered father say ' by Heaven ! ' lots o' times, but I don't know where 'tis."

For a moment the child looked up at him with wondering eyes, then answered,—

" Heaven's up in the sky, where God is, an' there ain't no hungry childer there, nor no cold, and everybody's 'appy, an' all the good people goes there when they die."

It was now Joe's turn to be astonished, and during the delivery of this speech his eyes kept growing wider and wider. At length he asked, " How did you get to know all that ? "

"Mother told me," was the answer, and the child burst out crying again.

"But if your mother's happy, like you say, you shouldn't cry," Joe said.

"I wouldn't cry if I could go, too," she answered, still sobbing; "but you don't know what 'tis to have nobody left, likely."

"No, I don't know what that is," Joe replied; and then silence fell between them. She still sat at Joe's feet, and every now and then he stroked her soft hair, and wondered what would become of her, and what he could do to help her.

At length, when her sobbing ceased again, he said, very gently,—

"What is your name, little girl?"

"Daisy Mary Blake," she answered quickly.

"Well, that is a pretty name!" he said. "Did your mother call you Daisy reg'lar?"

"Aye, she always called me Daisy."

"Then I'll call you Daisy, too, if you'll let me."

"But you'll be goin' away soon?" she asked.

"Aye, likely," he said thoughtfully.

"An' so shall I," she replied. "Mother tell'd me lots o' times as how when she went to heaven I should go to live in the country with Aunt Jane."

"Where 'bouts in the country?" Joe asked.

"Dunno," she replied; "but it's on the letter in the box. Can you read writin'?"

But Joe only shook his head. Such a question was beyond him altogether; and as neither of them had any further questions to ask, silence fell between them once more.

So the moments dragged slowly along, while they waited there alone with the dead until the morning should dawn. The daylight seemed a long time in coming, but it began to struggle through the fog at length ; and when it was sufficiently light Joe hobbled forth, with the aid of the dead woman's crutches, to call the neighbours, and bring them to the rescue of the little girl.

CHAPTER III.

A FRIEND IN NEED.

"Small service is *true* service while it lasts—
 Of humblest friends, bright creature, scorn not one
The daisy, by the shadow which it casts,
 Protects the lingering dewdrop from the sun."
                                —WORDSWORTH.

DURING the next two or three days Joe's feelings were of a very mixed character. To begin with, his parents did not return, and so his anxiety on their account steadily increased. Had it been his father only that had kept away he would not have troubled very much, for he had never been given to studying anyone's convenience but his own, nor had he ever manifested any very strong affection for either wife or child. But his mother was of very different disposition. Joe knew very well that he was the very apple of her eye; that it was the greatest joy of her life to have him near her, and that only some extraordinary circumstance could keep them apart.

As a consequence, Joe lavished all the affection of his nature on his mother. She was his all; hence her absence casued him the acutest anxiety and grief. Under the circumstances it was, perhaps, a fortunate thing that he became acquainted with Daisy Blake. Her great bereavement made him forgetful, to some extent, of his own troubles, and in trying to assuage her grief he found the truest balm for his own heart-aches.

Yet there were moments when he felt terribly depressed, and half disposed to give up heart and hope, and lie down and die. Each day his foot got more painful, until the mere act of lifting it from the ground made him almost shriek with agony. Added to that, he was almost famished for want of food, and he had not the courage to ask Daisy, or any of the friends that came to her rescue, for a crust of bread, and they had no suspicion that he was in need; while, to crown all his misery, the house-agent had given him notice to quit the miserable room he occupied and seek lodgings elsewhere.

It was in vain that Joe pleaded for a few days, grace, assuring the agent that he expected his parents home every minute.

" I've got too well used to stories of that sort," was the reply, " so don't imagine, lad, that you are going to fool me; and if you are not a fool yourself you'll not depend upon them any longer, and, indeed, you are quite big enough and old enough to shift for yourself."

This speech almost took Joe's breath away. Did the man mean that his parents had purposely forsaken him—left him to shift for himself as best he could? Before he could reply the agent went on,—

"I'll give you till to-morrow evening to clear out, but not an hour longer will you stay."

Joe heard these words with feelings akin to despair; and when the agent had gone, he lay down on the floor in that cheerless, fireless room, and burst into tears. Never had he known life so dark as it was just then; never had he felt so ill. If there had been a glass in the room he would have been astonished to see how pale and hollow-eyed he had got to look. He had been without food now two whole days, and without fire also. True, he had spent a large part of those days with his new acquaintance in the little room across the way, where they talked together almost in a whisper, as if afraid of waking the child's mother that slept in the room above, to which she had been taken.

But when night came on, Daisy went away with a neighbour who kept a little shop two blocks away, and who had promised to take care of her till her aunt from the country came to claim her; while poor Joe returned to his dark cheerless room, to lie awake the greater part of the night, and imagine unspeakable horrors that had overtaken his mother.

The misery of those nights no tongue could tell. He felt sometimes as though he would lose his reason, and in his heart wished that he might die. Daisy was his only comfort now, and his only friend. But even her friendship would soon come to an end. On the morrow her mother was to be taken away to the silent churchyard, and then the house would be shut up, and Daisy would come there no more. On the morrow, too,—unless his parents returned,—he was to be turned, hungry and helpless, into the streets to perish of want and cold.

"Well, what did it matter?" he said to himself as he lay there on the cold floor in utter misery and despair. It could scarcely be colder in the streets than in that dismal room.

"I may as well die in one place as another," he moaned. "I wish 'twere me they were a-buryin' instead o' Daisy's mother."

In his misery he forgot the flight of time, forgot the cold, forgot almost his hunger and pain. Even Daisy no longer occupied a place in his thoughts. So the minutes dragged slowly along until a full hour had passed, then the door was pushed slowly open, and a light footfall sounded on the threshold. But Joe did not heed it. He had given way again to another burst of tears, and was sobbing as though his heart would break.

For a moment Daisy stood irresolute, not knowing what to do. She had come across in search of him, much wondering what had kept him so long. In her grief she had found him her only comfort. He had seemed to her so kind and strong, and so full of cheerfulness and hope, that she felt quite miserable when he was out of sight.

Hence she stood aghast, when she stood on the threshold of that miserable room, and saw her strong hopeful friend lying sobbing on the floor. In a moment she grasped the truth, for she was quick-witted for her years, and wondered that she had not found out the truth before. How unselfish he had been, trying his best to ease her trouble, and yet all the while hiding his own; and for a moment her heart smote her with such a stab of pain as she had scarcely ever felt before. Then walking up to where he lay, she laid her hand gently on his head, and said softly,—

"What is the matter, Joe?"

"Is that you, Daisy?" Joe answered, with a start, hastily brushing away his tears at the same time.

"Yes, Joe; I comed to look for you, you've been so long. Be you in trouble?"

"Aye, Daisy, but I dunno want to vex you with it; you've trouble 'nough o' your own."

"Oh, Joe, an' I thought you were so 'appy!" said Daisy reproachfully.

"Happy, Daisy? No, I reckon I never shan't be happy till I'm dead," and Joe brushed his hand across his eyes again, to wipe away the tears that sprang into them.

"I wish you'd tell me your trouble, Joe," said Daisy quietly; "p'raps I could help yer."

"Nay, Daisy, 'twould on'y vex yer, and make yer more sorry."

For a moment Daisy was foiled, but she made up her mind she would not be defeated. So she changed her tactics.

"Aint yer cold, Joe?" she asked at length.

"Aye, awful," said Joe impulsively, "an' hunger'd too."

"Why don't yer light the fire, then, an' cook yer vittels?"

"'Cause I aint got———." Then Joe stopped suddenly, and tried to avoid Daisy's steady gaze.

For several moments neither spoke again. It was all plain enough to Daisy now. She did not want him to say any more. His confusion revealed all she wanted to know, and again her heart smote her for what seemed to her her great selfishness.

Daisy was the first to speak.

"Won't yer come across an' stay with me a little while, Joe?" she asked.

"Aye, I'll be very glad, Daisy, if I can get across; but my foot's awful to-day."

"I'll tell Mrs. Marks," said Daisy, "'an she'll make it better.

"Yer needn't bother nobody," said Joe; "I don't want to trouble folk."

"All right," said Daisy; but she meant, all the same, to get Mrs. Marks to look at his gathered heel.

A few minutes later Joe was sitting in a comfortable rocking-chair that belonged to Daisy's mother, while Daisy carefully mended the fire till it crackled cheerfully in the grate. The room seemed to Joe a perfect little palace after the desolate apartment he had just left, for Daisy's mother had not been poor as the people of Angel's Court understood poverty. Nor had she wasted her little savings during a long sickness, for, as we have seen, her death came suddenly through heart disease, so that plenty of food and fuel were found in the house after her death, and sufficient money to bury her decently.

When Daisy had got the fire burning to her satisfaction, she retired to a little pantry underneath the stairs, while Joe sat gazing vacantly at the glowing coals in the grate.

"Now then, I'm a-goin' to give 'im a s'prise," Daisy said to herself. "An' won't he stare when he sees what I've a got, that's all;" and Daisy smiled complacently, forgetting for the moment her own grief and loss in the thought of befriending one more desolate than herself.

CHAPTER IV.

NEVER MORE."

> " But in rejoicing with the glad,
>   The troubles of *our lot,*—
> Self—with its murmurs and its wants—
>   Must be, in love, forgot."

BEFORE Joe had any suspicion of what Daisy was doing, she had placed a large plate of bread and butter, cut thin, and several pieces of bun loaf, on a little round table, and pushed it close up to his rocking-chair, as he sat looking abstractedly into the fire.

He had been too busy with his own gloomy thoughts to notice her movements; but when he

I

caught sight of the food she had prepared for him, his eyes grew moist in a moment, and his lips trembled so that he could not speak. He was almost ravenous with hunger, and yet he felt as though it would be a cruel thing to eat the food of the orphan child; but he was too weak, too much overcome by Daisy's kindness to protest. And yet for the moment he knew if he attempted to eat, the food would choke him. Daisy noticed his hesitancy, and perhaps understood the reason, for she said to him, in her pleasantest fashion,—

"Now, Joe, you mustn't say nothin', not a word, till you've eat your dinner."

That was the last straw. Either the words, or the tone in which they were spoken, or perhaps both combined, broke him down completely, and, laying his forehead on the table, he burst into tears. The weakness was only momentary, however. Before Daisy had time to decide what to say or do, Joe raised his swimming eyes to his little friend, and said brokenly,—

"You *are* good, Daisy; and I'll never be able to thank yer proper."

"I don't want no thanks, Joe," was the gentle answer, "so don't say nothin' no more till you've eat yer dinner."

"Some day, p'raps, Daisy, I may have the chance to be good to you," Joe replied, without heeding Daisy's request; and then, as she made him no further answer, he proceeded to do ample justice to his dinner.

Daisy watched him for a moment, then set to work

to get him something to drink as well. And when he had finished, and declared that "he could eat no more if the house were full," she came and sat on a low stool at his feet, as she had done at the first.

For a few minutes there was silence between them. Then Daisy raised her eyes to his, and said simply,—

"You'll tell me yer trouble now, won't yer, Joe?"

"I'd rather not vex yer with my worries," Joe answered; "you've plenty o' trouble o' yer own."

"It'll vex me more not to know," she answered.

"It's very queer o' you," Joe replied; "ye're sich a little mite of a girl, an' talks like a woman."

"But I'm ten," said Daisy, drawing herself up proudly.

"I didn't think ye were so much," said Joe; "but I'm turned twelve, an' a head taller than you."

"You're a boy," was the answer; and Daisy looked as though she had settled the matter.

Perhaps Joe thought so too, for he no longer hesitated about telling her the story of his life. She did not interrupt him, so he went on quietly, recounting his experiences in town and country until he came to the events of the last few days; then he hesitated for a moment, but only for a moment. He felt, now that he had told so much, he might as well tell the whole.

Daisy listened in silence till he came to the conversation with the house-agent, then she burst out with an indignant exclamation.

"It can't be helped," said Joe. "If mother 'ud come home, or if my foot was well, I wouldn't mind. But I'll be able to shift some road; or if not, I can——

" Can what, Joe ? " Daisy asked, after a long pause.

" Well, I can die, Daisy."

" Oh no, Joe, yer mustn't say that," Daisy answered quickly.

" 'Twon't matter much, I'm thinkin'," Joe said gloomily. " I fear mother's dead, or she'd been back or sent word afore this ; so what's the odds ? "

But Daisy did not answer. Joe's words had made her think again of her own mother, and she was crying softly to herself.

So, with intervals of silence, they conversed together, chiefly about themselves, and ere the short November day faded in darkness they felt as though they had known each other all their lives. Daisy felt that in this big sun-browned lad she had found a true friend, while Joe felt that if he might be Daisy's protector he would still have something in life worth living for.

Mrs. Marks called to fetch away Daisy just as it was growing dusk, and, at Daisy's request, poulticed Joe's bad foot ; and then Joe hobbled across to his own dark and cheerless room, and wore away the dismal hours till sleep stole over him in trying to live over again the pleasant moments he had spent with his little friend.

On the following day Mrs. Blake was laid to rest in the grave. Daisy was the only mourner, for her Aunt Jane had not yet put in an appearance, nor sent any communication in reply to the letter that had been forwarded to her.

Joe spent the day in his own cheerless room, without food or fire. As the afternoon waned, hope died out of his heart, for every moment now he expected the house-agent ; and when at length the door opened, he quite expected to hear his stern voice bidding him go. It was quite a relief, therefore, when Daisy's gentle voice greeted him instead, and, springing up, he exclaimed, " You *are* good, Daisy ! "

" Be I ? " she said, simply. " But what do yer think I've been thinkin', Joe ? "

" Dunno," Joe answered, with a look of curiosity on his face.

" Well, then, I've been thinkin' that, if yer wouldn't be skear'd, yer might sleep in our house."

" Sleep in your house ? " said Joe, wonderingly.

" Aye, Joe, if yer wouldn't mind. Mother paid her rent every month, an' Mrs. Marks says mother's time's not up for nine or ten days yet."

Joe gave a low whistle at this information, but made no further answer.

" I was 'fraid ye'd be skeared," Daisy said after a long pause.

" Me skear'd ! " Joe exclaimed ; " not if I knows it. But how'm I to get in ? 'cause I see Mrs. Marks lock the door after you'd all come out this afternoon, and put the key in her pocket."

" Aye, but there's two keys ! " said Daisy, with a knowing look. " Mother always kep' one, and I th' other, an' I've brought my key for you."

" Glorious ! " said Joe, " that's just the ticket. Daisy, you're a brick, an' I'll never be able to thank yer 'nough as long as I live."

" An' in the pantry, Joe, there's some bread an' cake," Daisy continued, " an' there's plenty o' coal

to keep a good fire; an' to-morrow mornin' I'll be up
fust thing."

Joe found all that Daisy said, and that night he
slept more soundly than he had done for several
nights past. True to her promise, Daisy came to see
him in the morning, and spent the greater part of the
day in his company.

"Aunt Jane aint turned up yet," she said; "an' I
don't care if she don't come till Christmas."

"I wish she wouldn't come at all," said Joe.

"Why d' yer say that?" asked Daisy, in surprise.

"'Cause when you goes, I shan't have nobody left,"
Joe said.

"But you'll be going away when your foot gets
better, won't yer?" she asked.

"Aye, I s'pose so," Joe answered. "I wish we
could both go together."

"Oh, but you'll be able to come to see me, won't
yer?"

"Aye, if I live, I will."

That night the gathering that had given Joe so
much pain broke; and next morning, when Daisy
called, he felt, he said, as light as a lark.

They had a long talk together that day, the last
they ever had in that little room. Since that night
when Daisy's mother died, Joe had greatly puzzled
himself respecting what she had said about heaven,
and the more he had thought about the matter the
more mystified he had become.

Daisy was only too delighted to show off her
superior knowledge. To her simple faith everything
was clear and plain; and so she told Joe in simple

language all she knew. Joe listened with wide-open eyes while she told him how God was everywhere, and saw everything; how He was very good, and hated sin; how lying and swearing, stealing, and getting drunk were very wicked, and grieved the good God that loved us all; how Christ had come— God's only Son—to die for us, and take away our sin; and how good people would be happy here, and go to a happy place when they died; and how bad people would be miserable here, and hereafter as well.

Most of this was new to Joe. Hints of these truths his mother had given him from time to time, but nothing definite had ever been taught him; and so Daisy's words came to him like a revelation, filling him with wonder and awe.

Soon after noon Daisy went back to Mrs. Marks' to dinner, and Joe stood in the doorway, and watched her tripping lightly down the court. "They must ha' called this place Angel's Court after Daisy," was his thought, for verily she seemed an angel to this poor, sad-hearted lad.

"I'll come back in the evenin', Joe," were her last words to him, and she tripped lightly away. Ah! little did he think that only in his dreams was he to hear that voice again; that never more would her presence brighten Angel's Court; that never more would she come back to him in that little room!

CHAPTER V.

ADRIFT.

"Down through the line of the rolling years,
 No shirking the just decree,
The dire fulfilment each day appears
 Abroad on both earth and sea ;
Life's fears and troubles, and ills, and tears,
 Cling round us in unity."—Florence Dudley.

SCARCELY had Daisy disappeared round the corner than Joe took the crutches already referred to, and hobbled forth into the court. His foot, to use his own expression, "was mendin' bravely," and he was anxious to look about him so that he might form some idea as to how he was to earn his living.

He had almost given up hope of his parents' return, while to depend on Daisy's charity any longer than he could possibly help he was resolved not to do.

He knew a little about chair and umbrella mending, and if it came to a pinch he could do a little tinkering; so that he was not without hope that he might find employment somewhere, and earn enough to keep him from absolute starvation.

It did not take him long to get out of Angel's Court, and turning to the right he soon found himself in a busy thoroughfare, but leading he knew not whither. He was careful, however, to take particular notice of the streets, so that he might find his way back again.

To most people the neighbourhood would not be considered inviting, but Joe pronounced it "just the ticket." A number of cellar shops, where tinkers, cobblers, and toymakers were at work, inspired him with the hope that he would be able to obtain employment sooner or later, though before the afternoon closed round him that hope had been considerably dimmed, and when he hobbled back to Angel's Court he was half disposed to give way to despair.

However, Daisy would be coming to see him directly, or perhaps was already waiting for hin; so for her sake he would have to put the best face on the matter he could, and try to look the bright side of things— if there was a bright side—which he very much doubted.

He was half expecting that Daisy would meet him at the door. In that, however, he was disappointed.

"Any road, she's been 'ere !" was his exclamation,

as soon as he had got a light; " but what in the name o' Methusler has she been a-pullin' the furniture round arter this fashion for ? "   And Joe set to work to put the room straight again.   That somebody had been in during his absence was an absolute certainty, and if he had looked a little more closely he would have discovered that several things had been taken away.   He never suspected, however, that any one but Daisy could have entered the house, so, after he had mended the fire, he said to himself,—

" Bless that little gal ! shouldn't a' wonder if she wer'n't a-hidin' somewhere, an' is goin' to try an' skear me ; " and Joe looked cautiously into the little pantry, but Daisy was not there.   He found half a loaf of bread, however, which he proceeded to attack in a vigorous fashion, and when he had satisfied his appetite he sat down to wait for Daisy's coming.

" Bless the little gal ! " he said every now and then to himself, " she's a bonny 'un an' no mistake, but I wish she'd make haste."

As the evening wore away and Daisy did not come, he went out and stood in the doorway, and looked long and eagerly down the smoky court, and wondered much what could have kept her.

He was afraid to go in search of her lest she should come during his absence, and, finding the house empty, go back again.

So the minutes dragged slowly along, and lengthened into hours, and still he stood in the doorway waiting, waiting, while a dark foreboding kept eating its way into his heart, with a pain that was almost unbearable

At length, when fire and candle had both burned themselves out, and darkness suddenly filled the little room, he turned away with a great sob, and without troubling himself to lock the door, he threw himself on the bed and gave way to a flood of tears.

"Oh, Daisy! oh, mother!" was his cry. Both had gone away from him promising that they would return again in the evening, and both had failed to return when evening came. He had expected his mother would return with the first streak of the morning, but he had watched and waited in vain. Would he watch and wait in vain for Daisy also? He feared so, for something in his heart whispered to him that she would return no more.

The long dreary night came to an end at length, and, throwing open the door, he went and stood in the doorway again. He could see nothing, however, for the fog had come on again, and was more dense than ever. Yet, notwithstanding this, he kept staring into the fog for more than an hour, and then, half-frozen with cold, he went back into the room and commenced to light the fire. About noon he ate what food remained in the little pantry, and then began to debate with himself what course he should adopt.

But for the fear of missing her, he would have gone in search of her long before this. He did not know exactly where Mrs. Marks lived, but he had no doubt he could find out.

Most likely Mrs. Marks would ask him what business he had troubling about Daisy Blake, and would perhaps send him away without answering his questions. But he was resolved, nevertheless, if Daisy

did not put in an appearance before dark, to go in
search of her.

So the afternoon wore away, till the short November
day began to fade, when he was startled by the sound
of strange voices outside the door; the next moment
the door was thrown open, and two men walked into
the room.

Joe had been sitting on the bed looking vacantly
into the fire, but at their entrance started to his feet
in a moment.

"Hullo, you young wagabond!" said one of the men,
starting back for the moment as though he had seen
an apparition, the next moment rushing forward and
seizing Joe by the collar. "What d'yer mean by
thieving here?"

"I'm not thievin'," said Joe, stoutly. "I'm a-wait-
ing for Daisy."

"Waitin' for Daisy, eh?" said the man, with a
great laugh.

"Aye, I be," said Joe, "an' you've no leave to be
here without her knowin'. It's you that's doin' the
thievin'."

"What's that, you young scoundrel?" said the man,
shaking Joe by the collar as a terrier might shake a
rat. "You'd better dry up, or I'll hand you over to the
pleece."

"I've as much right here as you," replied Joe, "an'
likely a deal more."

"Come, ye'd better hook it," said the man, "'an say
no more. This furniter is ourn; we've bought the lot,
and we ain't going to have young vagrants like you
loitering about; so hook it without another word."

"I b'leeve ye're a-lyin'," said Joe, making a rush for the door to escape a kick that was aimed at him by the infuriated broker.

Once in the court, Joe felt it his duty to go and inform Daisy of what was taking place. By dint of a little inquiry he was not long in finding Mrs. Marks' shop, and pushing open the door he found himself face to face with that good woman.

"Please, Mrs. Marks," said Joe, eagerly, "is Daisy here?"

"No, she aint," was the reply; "why do you ax?"

"'Cause there's two men at her house takin' away the furniter."

"Oh, that's quite right; they've bought 'em."

"Bought 'em?" echoed Joe, scarcely crediting his own ears.

"Aye, Daisy's uncle comed over yesterday an' got a broker to take the lot at a waliation."

"And where's Daisy?" said Joe, eagerly.

"Gone back wi' her uncle, to be sure; where d'ye think she were a-goin' to be?"

"I didn't know as she 'ad a huncle," said Joe, after an awkward pause.

"Well, then, yer knows it now," said the woman. "Her aunt were too ill to fetch her, so her uncle comed instead."

"An' where's he taken her to?" said Joe.

"Well, you're a mighty inquisitive boy," said Mrs. Marks, looking hard at Joe; "an' I don't know as 'ow it can be any business o' yourn as to where the gal is; but all the same I don't know myself. It's some-

where t'other side o' Wigan, I b'leeve, and that's all I
knows; so good evenin'.'"

For a moment Joe stood as if petrified; then, rousing hinself, he hobbled slowly to the door, and without
a word passed out into the wintry street. All his
worst fears were realized. Daisy had gone, never to
return again. Her little home was in the possession
of strangers, and he was adrift in the night, without
shelter and without a friend.

For a while Joe hobbled aimlessly on through the
murky streets. He had no fear about losing his way
now, for one place was the same to him as another.

At length he stumbled across a lad of about his
own age, who was seated on a doorstep with his legs
stretched half across the narrow way.

'Hullo, crutches!'" called the stranger, " where ye a
drivin' to?"

"Anywheres," said Joe, moodily.

"Down in the mouth, eh?"

"Aye," said Joe, "but what are ye a-doin' there;
sprawlin' yer legs all over the pavement?"

"Watchin' for game," was the answer. "Are ye in
for a bit o' honest work?"

"Aye, that I be " said Joe, eagerly. "Do yer know
of anything?"

"Aye, plenty. What's yer name, an' where d'ye
live?"

"I don't live nowhere," said Joe. "Mother an'
father aint turned up for four days, and I aint nowhere to go: my name's Joe Bradley."

"And mine's Swivel," answered the other, "nothing
but Swivel. I don't belong to nobody, aint got no

"Hullo, Crutches! where ye drivin' to?

foather nor mother, never 'ad. I were 'atched in the
workus, an' here I be, a credit to my trainin'. You
come wi' me, Joe, and I'll put you up to a thing or
two as honest as moonshine. Splendiferous night,
this! bobbies can't see the length o' their ugly mugs.
You come wi' me." And he started up the street at a
brisk walk; and Joe, much wondering, followed.

K

CHAPTER VI.

CAUGHT.

"Sowing the seed of a lingering pain,
Sowing the seed of a maddened brain,
Sowing the seed of a tarnished name,
Sowing the seed of eternal shame,
Oh, what shall the harvest be?"

COME, hurry hup, Crutches!" said Swivel, after he had gone some little distance. Then, pausing a few moments, he said:

"I beg your parding, Joe, but I forgot yer name for the moment. I likes the name, for it's got a honest ring 'bout it, an' I allers feels frien'ly to honest boys like myself, who is a-fightin' again' a 'ard world 'an a-tryin' to live square."

This was said with such an air of sincerity that

Joe's heart quite warmed towards his new acquaintance, and he continued to follow without the least
misgiving.

After many twists and turns, they found themselves mounting a flight of rickety stairs, at the top of
which was a long, dimly-lighted room. Here some
ten or dozen lads were gathered, and, judging from
the noise they made, were in a very happy frame of
mind.

Joe was welcomed in a boisterously-friendly fashion,
and Swivel was congratulated on finding and bringing
home another " poor lost lamb."

Joe was not altogether satisfied with the company
in which he found himself, and yet he could discover
no particular reason why. Most of the lads were
about his own age. All were ragged, and several of
them were dirty. Yet they were all good-humoured
and frolicsome, and there was not one of them that
was not disposed to be on friendly terms with him.
But for all that, Joe was not altogether at his ease.

Swivel was not slow in noting that fact, and so
proceeded to set Joe at his ease by explaining matters.

" This ere place, Joe," he said, " is a horphan's
'ome, where pore horphans whose parients is in quod
or elsewhere is a-pertected from the world's wintry
blastes. We all arns our livin' in the honestest way
possible, and looks out at the same time for pore stray
lambs like yerself, to keep 'em hout o' temptation."

" Now, Billy," he said, turning to a red-headed lad
with an awful squint, " sing us one o' yer hymns, so as
our new frien' may see 'ow 'ligious we are."

Billy, being thus appealed to, rolled his eyes up to

the ceiling, and commenced in an ear-splitting voice to
sing :

> " I want to be a hangel,
> An' with the hangels stan',
> A crown upon my for'yed,
> An 'arp widin my 'and. "

" There now, Joe," said Swivel; " yer see now
what good 'ligious stuff we're made of, and 'ow we
means to be frien's to yer."

" Well," said Joe, feeling a little more at his ease,
" ye are very kind, an' I'm much obliged to yer."

" Oh, don't mention it !" said Swivel, who seemed
to be the spokesman of the party. " We wants to
'elp yer, if we can. What yer say now to bein' one o'
our little band ? "

" Dunno," said Joe. " What do ye do ? "

" Oh, anything as "—

But here Swivel's speech was interrupted by the
entrance of a young man of some twenty-two or three
years of age, who glanced swiftly round the room, and
caught sight of Joe in a moment.

" A new recruit, eh ? " he said, as if speaking to
himself.

" Aye," said Swivel. I found 'im in Mill Street,
elpless an' unpertected, an' brought 'im 'ome."

" Quite right, Swivel; and now he is ready to join
our band. Is that right, my young friend ? " he said,
turning to Joe.

" Aye," said Joe, beginning to feel uncomfortable
again. " I ain't no place to go, an' I wants to get a
honest livin' somewheres."

" Quite right," was the reply ; " nothing like being

honest," and he turned his head to hide a sneer that curled his lips.

"Now, lads, sing us that new ditty you learned at the meeting the other day ; " and in a moment they started, Billy's voice leading the rest :

> " Dare to be a Dan'yel,
> Dare to stan' alone ;
> Dare to 'ave a purpus, lads,
> An' never make it known."

" Of course you go to meeting ? " said the young man, turning to Joe.

But Joe only shook his head.

" How sad ? " he continued. " Nor to church nor chapel ? "

Another shake of the head.

" What ! not religiously brought up ? "

" Don't know what that is," said Joe.

" Ah ! I see how it is," he went on. " Education sadly neglected. But all the better ; you'll have nothing to unlearn, and we'll make a man of you."

" Thank yer," said Joe, not knowing what else to say.

" Oh, don't mention it," was the reply. " It's our mission to help the friendless, but on one condition : and that is, that for the first week you just do what you are told, and ask no questions. Will you promise that ? " and he looked Joe straight in the eyes.

" Aye," said Joe, trembling all over, " I promise yer."

" That'll do," he said ; " and as Swivel found you, you are to be his pall for the first week."

Joe nodded his head.

" You'll look after him, Swivel ? "

" Aye, Captain," Swivel answered with a leer;
' you may trust me for that."

" Now, then, let the supper come on, and then
prepare for business ; " saying which, he marched out
of the room.

Joe felt more comfortable when he had departed, and
hobbled up to Swivel with the question, " Who's he."

" Oh, he's the Captain ! " said Swivel, looking important.   " He's a mighty big man, bigger'n' the
peelers, or anybody.   We've all of us jist to do what
he tells us ; if we don't, he could clap us in jail in no
time.   You keep the right side o' 'im, an' you're right."

" Oh, indeed ! " said Joe.

" But," said Swivel, " you're to ax no more questions
to-night, but jist do what I tells yer.   But 'ere's the
supper."

This was brought into the room in a basket by an
old woman they designated " Mother " ; and if the meal
was not particularly toothsome, it was at least abund-
ant, and Joe was by no means backward in doing
ample justice to the repast.

It was near midnight when he sauntered forth into
the foggy street, accompanied by Swivel, much wondering what kind of work could be on hand at such
an unearthly hour.

" Splendiferous night, this ! " said Swivel ; " no
peelers about, or, if they be, they can't see us.   Now,
keep your weather-heye hopen, Joe, an' foller me."

Remembering his instructions, Joe followed without
making any remark or asking a single question.

At length they paused in a narrow entry.

"Now, you wait 'ere, Joe," said Swivel, "while I gets over and unbolts the yard-door."

To unbolt the door was the work of a moment, and Joe felt himself pulled by Swivel into the yard.

"Don't speak," said Swivel in a whisper. "The lad as runs arrands here 'as been tipped to leave the window unfastened. Now, come an' 'elp to lift."

Remembering his promise, Joe reluctantly obeyed, for he had a feeling that he was being led into a trap.

"Bother the noise!" said Swivel. "Now, foller me;" and Joe quickly followed through the half-open window.

Once in the room, Swivel produced a small lamp which had been hidden under his jacket, and Joe saw that he was in a shop of some kind.

"A lot o' perwisions has been left 'ere for the horphans," whispered Swivel. "It looks like stealin', maybe, to you, but it ain't. Now stuff these cakes inter yer pockets."

Again Joe obeyed, but with great reluctance, for he did not feel quite certain that Swivel was telling the truth.

"Hist!" whispered Swivel, "what's that noise?"

The next moment a door was thrown open, and a man rushed into the room. Swift as a flash of lightning (so it seemed to Joe) Swivel disappeared through the open window, and was soon lost in the fog. But Joe, with his lame foot, was by no means rapid in his movements, and almost before he could recover his astonishment found himself a prisoner. A few minutes later he was marched by a policeman to the lock-up, not at all certain whether he was awake or dreaming.

He had plenty of time, however, for reflection in the weeks that followed. The trial before the magistrates on the following morning was of the briefest and most formal character. He had been caught red-handed in the act ; and with very little ado, he was sentenced to two months' imprisonment.

When the sentence was pronounced, Joe cast a hurried glance round the room before the policeman marched him away. But in the sea of faces that met his, he saw one face only, and that the face of Swivel. It was but a momentary glance, but it filled him with indignation. There was no pity in Swivel's face, nor sorrow, nor sympathy. On the contrary, Joe saw that he was laughing at his discomfiture. The hideous grin upon his face haunted him for days, and angered him almost to madness.

" I'll be even with him yet ! " he said, with clenched fists. " If ever I meet him again, I'll not leave him with a sound bone in his skin ! "

Joe had been reared in almost total ignorance of religious truth. That he should live honestly had been the highest, and indeed the only, rule of his life. That much his mother had taught him by precept and example, but rather as a matter of policy than anything else.

Yet Joe was not destitute of moral sense. He had an inborn hatred of meanness and treachery, and an inborn respect also for the rights of others. He knew it would be wrong for anyone to take what was his, and so easily arrived at the conclusion that it would be equally wrong for him to take what belonged to another.

In some instances he had not been able to see where the rights of others came in, and so had been kept in the right path only by the fear of punishment. He had associated "jail" with the idea of constant whippings, and so was greatly relieved when he discovered that he was not to be whipped at all. The idea of "disgrace" did not enter his head, and about the only trying part of the punishment was the confinement; and as the days passed away he grew almost reconciled to that, especially as he remembered that liberty only meant to him hunger, and cold, and destitution.

CHAPTER VII.

ON THE TRAMP.

" Has sorrow thy young days shaded,
    As clouds o'er the morning fleet ?
Too fast have those young days faded,
    That, even in sorrow, were sweet ?
Does time with its cold wing wither
    Each feeling that once was dear ?
Then, child of misfortune, come hither ;
    I'll weep with thee tear for tear."

—MOORE.

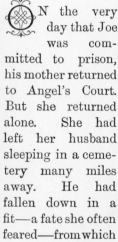

ON the very day that Joe was committed to prison, his mother returned to Angel's Court. But she returned alone. She had left her husband sleeping in a cemetery many miles away. He had fallen down in a fit—a fate she often feared—from which he never rallied. For two days and nights she never left his bedside, and then he quietly breathed out his spirit into the hands of God.

Sending a message to Joe by a pedlar of her acquaintance, she waited till after the funeral, and then returned to Angel's Court, hungering for a sight of her boy, who was now more than ever "her all." She never dreamed that the pedlar would neglect to deliver her message. Hence her grief and consternation were pitiful to witness when she discovered the house empty, and her child nowhere to be found. Up and down the court she ran, in a state bordering on frenzy, calling, "Joe! Joe!"

From several of the neighbours she learned that he had been seen on the previous day, but no one had taken any notice of his movements, or could give any information as to his whereabouts. Mrs. Marks was able to give the most definite account, but it led to nothing. And after waiting in the neighbourhood for nearly a week without being able to glean any tidings of her boy, she started again for the country.

"He never could abide the towns," she said to herself; "perhaps I'll find him yet on some of the old tracks;" and shouldering her bundle of canes, she marched away, resolving that she would never give up the search, though she had to tramp the country over.

Meanwhile Joe wore away the dreary winter days in his prison cell. Nor were they profitless days to him.

In the chaplain of the jail he found a true friend, who took an interest in him from the first, and readily believed Joe's straightforward story.

"It's a good thing you were caught the very first night," he said to Joe a few days after his committal.

"How d'yer make that out?" Joe asked.

"Because, had you gone on a week without detection you would have found yourself completely in the hands of those sharpers. You would have discovered that you were one of a band of thieves, that you had actually taken part in their operations, and hence were no better than they. And so, losing your self-respect, you would have little inducement to leave their company: very likely would be afraid to attempt it; or, what is quite as likely, would have got to enjoy the excitement and danger of such a life."

"And so every bit they told me about the orphan home was a lie?" said Joe.

"Every bit of it, my lad. They saw that you were an honest lad, and so all that talk was just a blind. It is sad to think of, but it is to be feared that there are many such bands of juvenile thieves in this great city."

"If I once get hold of Swivel again!" said Joe, "I'll pound him to a jelly!"

"You have more to fear from a meeting with him than he has. Very likely he and some of his comrades will be on the look-out for you when you leave this place. I must try to get you away a day before your time, and then my advice is, go straight away from this place as fast as you can."

"What! without hidin' Swivel?"

"Yes, Joe; you remember what I read to you yesterday about forgiving your enemies?"

"Aye, I 'members; but it ain't much in my line."

"But you must ask God to help you," said the chaplain. And then followed a long earnest talk about the duty of forgiveness and the blessedness of doing good, which Joe never forgot to his dying day.

It was well on towards the middle of January when Joe found himself at liberty once more. His foot, too, was quite well, and in health and spirits he was better than he had been for many a long day past.

With a half-crown in his pocket, which the chaplain had given him, he took that good man's advice, and started straight for the country. The weather was fine, but bitterly cold, the whole country being locked in the grip of a fortnight's frost. But Joe rather rejoiced in that than otherwise; the roads were in capital condition for walking, and he had scarcely got a mile on his way before he found himself " as warm as toast," as he expressed it.

His destination was some unknown place " the other side of Wigan." To this nameless region Daisy had been taken, and, next to his mother, he cared more for her than anybody else in the world. If he could find Daisy, he thought, he would not be altogether desolate and alone. Not that he supposed she could help him in any way; but if he could keep near her, there might come a time when he could help her, and so discharge the big debt of gratitude he owed. Scarcely an hour had passed, since that morning he had watched her tripping down the court, but she had been in his thoughts. Even in his dreams she was with him, ever encouraging him to struggle on.

The first night of his tramp he crept into a barn, the door of which he found open, and lay down in a heap of straw. It was no new experience to him. He had often done it in the old days of wandering from place to place, and much preferred it to sleeping underneath the tent especially when the weather was at all cold.

The days of his childhood came very vividly back to him as he lay there alone; and yet they seemed separated from the present by an enormous distance of time. It seemed to him as if he had lived years in the last two months. No other part of his life was crowded so full of strange and painful experiences.

Then from the past his thoughts turned naturally to the future, and he had to confess to himself that the outlook was very dark. It seemed to him as if he were on a fool's errand. Suppose he found Daisy, what good would that do him? And even if it would do him good, what prospect had he of finding her with such a vague address? "The other side of Wigan" might mean almost anywhere. He did not even know the name of her relatives; and even if he *did* know their name, even if he discovered their place of residence, what then? And with these perplexing questions haunting him, he fell into a troubled sleep.

When he awoke in the morning he was stiff, cold, and hungry; but a brisk walk along the frozen road soon banished the stiffness and cold, though it considerably increased his hunger. So he turned aside into a village inn, and gave orders for a substantial breakfast. This lessened his small fortune by nine-pence; but as he "took aboard," as he said, sufficient to last him the whole day, the meal could not, in any sense, be considered dear.

That night Joe reached the town of Wigan, and spent the whole of his remaining fortune in supper, bed, and breakfast. He was not discouraged, however: in a few hours now he might reasonably expect to be "the other side of Wigan," and once let him feel that Wigan was behind him, and he would begin in sober earnest to search for employment. And if he could only get steady work, he would be able to institute inquiries in different directions, and so, perhaps, discover in time the object of his search. At the same time, he could be on the look-out for his parents, for, on the whole, he imagined he would be more likely to discover them remaining in one place than by tramping round the country.

So when Joe had been on the tramp a little over two hours, and was feeling that now Wigan was well behind him, he climbed to the top of a hill and looked round him. The country looked rather desolate in the pale slanting sunshine, and the cold wind chilled him almost to the marrow.

Behind him Wigan lay obscured in its own smoke. Right and left, hilly and broken country stretched as far as eye could reach, while in front was a broad plain of perfectly level country, fringed on its distant edge by the shining sea; and Joe felt that all this great stretch of country was the "beyond Wigan" of which he had been in search. And now, what should he do next?

"I'll begin at the beginnin'," he said; and off he started to the nearest farmhouse. and then to the next and next, and next, and ever with the same result. They wanted no lad, and, if they did, there were plenty of lads who were reared in the country, and knew all about farm-work. And so the day wore away, while disappointment incessantly dogged his steps, and hunger and weariness and cold crushed down his hopes and filled his eyes with tears.

He was now quite in the country, and darkness was coming on apace. He had never rested a moment since he started in the morning, nor had a morsel of food passed his lips. What should he do? This was the question that haunted him as he dragged himself wearily along the frozen road, and filled him almost with despair.

In the bare leafless trees that overhung the road here and there, the winter wind moaned and sighed as though in sympathy with his forlorn and pitiful state, while in the sky above his head the stars came out one by one, and seemed to look down upon him with pitying eye; but, alas! it was not pity he needed, but help, and that he could not find.

Still, on he trudged, but with failing strength. The daylight had all faded now, and only the light of the frosty stars showed him the way.

"It's of no use," he moaned to himself; "I can go no farther; an' I may as well die here as anywhere else;" and he staggered up against the hedge and threw himself full-length on the frozen grass."

"I'll be froze 'gin mornin'," he said, "an' out o' it all. An Daisy told me there's no cold in heaven."

Then it suddenly occurred to him that he ought to

pray. The chaplain had taught him a little prayer, which he had repeated every night while in the prison.

"I'll say it again for the last time, an' then I'll go to sleep."

CHAPTER VIII.

ELI HOLT.

"Listen how the bells are ringing
　　Out upon the air ;
List the worshippers' sweet singing,
　　Hear the fervent prayer
Like a sweet perfume ascending,
　　Up to One on high ;
With the angel anthems blending,
　　Full of harmony."
　　　　　—FLORENCE DUDLEY.

RAISING himself to his knees and clasping his hands in an attitude of supplication, Joe commenced the little prayer that he had been taught. But scarcely had the first sentence escaped his lips ere he paused suddenly.

What sound was that ?　Was it the ringing of church bells. to call worshippers to prayer

or was it a welcome home from the bells of heaven?
He had heard Daisy attempt to sing once or twice:

> " Ring the bells of heaven,
> There is joy to-day."

And perhaps these were heaven's bells he heard.

But, there! The music had ceased again, and all
was still once more, save for the swish of the wind in
the bare tree above his head; or perhaps it was not
the wind at all that he heard, only the rush of angels'
wings, who had come down to carry him to the better
country away up beyond the stars.

And Joe opened his eyes to look for the angels, but
quickly closed them again with a sigh. It was but
the wind after all, sighing through the bare branches
of the tree, and whistling among the frozen grasses
that fringed the hedge.

Then all of a sudden the bells rang out once more.
Ring, ting! ring, ting! and Joe started to his feet.
Down between the hedges of the lonely road the
music seemed to sweep, and passed onward into the
night; and to his dulled and drowsy sense it sounded
wonderfully sweet, and awoke within him a desire to
get nearer the source whence it came.

So, gathering up all his remaining strength, he
staggered into the road, and then started forward in
the direction from whence the music came. On! on!
still on! lured by the music of the bells. He saw no
road, he felt no cold; every sense but that of hearing
was dulled and dead, and while the music lasted he
could but go on.

Then suddenly he stopped. The bells had ceased,

and darkness and silence wrapped him in their folds once more. But only for a few moments.

"There they go again," he said. Ring, ting! ring, ting! ring, ting! And to his bewildered fancy it sounded to him as though a voice were calling, Come home! Come home! Come home! Nearer, too, and clearer the sounds rang out, filling him with courage and with hope. Surely never such welcome music was rung out on an anvil before!

A turn in the road and the secret was revealed, while from the blacksmith's forge a ruddy and welcome glare shone out across the way.

"He'll surely let me warm myself this bitter night," Joe said to himself; "any road, I'll ax," and he staggered forward, buoyed up with his last hope.

He did not wait to read the sign above the door, "Eli Holt, blacksmith." He did not notice the farm implements lying on the ground before the door. He had no eyes for anything but the glowing fire, and so, staggering blindly on, he caught his foot in a corner of a harrow and fell with a heavy thud upon the frozen ground. He felt a sharp spasm of pain dart through his head, then all became a blank. The fire blazed on, and crackled and roared as the blacksmith plied the bellows, while out on the frosty air the music of the anvil rang. But Joe neither saw the one nor heard the other. With a stone for his pillow at last, he lay, heedless of wind and cold.

Meanwhile Eli Holt went steadily on with his

work. Just at present he was more than usually busy for a big strong lad who had worked with him as an apprentice for the last twelve months had taken it into his head, only the day before, to run away to Liverpool for the purpose of going to sea.

It was rather tantalizing to Eli that the lad should run away just as he was beginning to get handy; however, he was not going to make a fuss about the matter. "If the lad wants to go to sea," he said, "let him go. One voyage will cure him, as it cured me when I was a lad."

So Eli went quietly on with his work, saying little to anybody, but thinking his own thoughts all the same. He was a very reliable man was Eli. Always at the shop when wanted, and never given to spending his evenings in the public-house, as is sometimes the case with those who work at the anvil and forge.

He had come to "Three Lanes End" more than ten years before from some village many miles away, and he had come alone; no wife or child kept him company. He had left his wife sleeping in the churchyard of the village he had left; and his only child—a daughter—was dead also. At least, she was dead to him. Gossip was not agreed on this question. Some people said he had buried her in the grave with his wife. Others said she was not dead at all. But—— and the sentence usually ended with a shake of the head.

Eli himself was silent on the question. He admitted that he had passed through great trouble,

that he had lost both wife and child, and so poignant
had been his grief that he felt he could no longer live
in the old home; and hearing that the business at
Three Lanes End was to be disposed of, he sold his
own and came and purchased this.

This was the extent of Eli's story, and no amount
of questioning could wring anything further from his
lips. In a very few weeks he proved himself to be a
good workman, honest, steady, and reliable, and so
found himself at all times with quite as much work
on hand as he wanted.

Eli lived quite alone in a neat little house adjoining
the smithy. A charwoman from the village came two
or three times a week to wash and mend and cook.
But though she was a noted gossip, she could never
get anything out of Eli. Excepting Sundays, he
only went into the house to eat and sleep, and on
Sundays he went regularly to Church, morning and
evening.

So the years sped along peacefully enough. He
seemed to find his greatest solace in his work, never
courting company, nor shunning it when it came.
Sometimes of a winter evening the smithy would be
full of labourers from the surrounding farms, and Eli
would take advantage of their presence to get some
heavy work done, such as "laying" a plough-share, or
putting a band on a cart-wheel.

Some of the young men were quite adepts at
swinging the heavy hammer, and Eli gave them
plenty of practice when they came to visit him.

On the evening, however, when Joe staggered and

fell before his door he was quite alone, and, on the whole, he was glad of it. He wanted a quantity of horse-shoe nails knocked off, and he could always accomplish that kind of work better when alone than when he had company. Moreover, it was a kind of work he liked; he could always think his best thoughts when his hammer was tinkling lightly on his anvil, and the red-hot nails dropped quickly on the floor. So he went on rapidly with his work, till the long pair of nail rods had been worked back to " stumps."

" I think I'll give over now," he said to himself, looking at his watch at the same time. " Aye, and it's quite time too;" and he went and bolted the window-shutters.

" Now for a pipe," he muttered to himself, " and then for bed." And filling his pipe, he went out to look at the weather before lighting it, which had become with him an invariable custom.

" Hullo!" he exclaimed, as he drew back suddenly from the prostrate form of Joe, that was lying right across his path; " what in the world is this?"

One glance, however, was sufficient to answer that question. The next moment he had Joe in his arms and was carrying him into the smithy.

" I fear it's all over with the lad," he muttered, as the dim firelight fell on Joe's white, drawn face. " Poor lad; he was somebody's boy. I wonder what he could be doing here."

The next minute he was lying before the fire, with Eli's apron under his head.

With his finger on his wrist, Eli watched him anxiously for several minutes, then, with a sigh, he turned away.

" It's too late," he said.   " This is a case for a ' crowner's ' jury."

CHAPTER IX.

A FRESH START.

"And when temptation's power was strong,
    And lured his heart to sin,
He sought the Holy Spirit's aid
    To make him pure within ;
That so he might, when death came nigh,
    Die calmly, as the righteous die."

—G. W. Brameld.

IN after years Joe described the events of that evening as the "nearest squeak he ever had in his life." "The dying was easy enough," he said, "but the coming to life again was ten thousand times worse than awful." It was near midnight before Eli succeeded in rousing him to full consciousness. and then, for several hours, he said it was as though a thousand red-hot needles were being run into every part of his body.

Seven or eight hours' unbroken sleep, however, on Eli's sofa, in front of a warm fire, worked wonders. It was nearly noon when he opened his eyes and looked eagerly around him, in a dazed, bewildered way. "Where, in the name o' Hobadiah, be I ?" he said to himself. "Gracious mercy! if I ain't been swaped for some other lad, I'm a Jew !" and he raised himself on his elbow to take a better look round him.

Just then the ring of Eli's hammer on the anvil brought suddenly back the events of the previous evening, and he lay back on the sofa again and closed his eyes.

"I wish he'd let me die," he said to himself, "for I'll 'ave to go on the tramp again, an' face the 'unger an' cold, an' I ain't no heart left;" and two big tears stole out under his eyelids and rolled slowly down his cheeks.

A few minutes later Eli came into the room to get his dinner, and Joe sprang up with a start, then sat down again, for he felt as yet very weak.

"Well, lad, and are ye better?" said Eli, in a kindly tone of voice.

"Oh, aye!" said Joe. "I'm a bit mazy an' a trifle limp about the knees; but I'll be able to get a bit farther, I reckon."

"Going far?" Eli asked.

"I'm on the look-out for a job," Joe answered. "I 'ad no luck 'esterday, but I must try again."

"What can ye do?" was Eli's next question.

"Not much, I fear," Joe answered in doleful tones; then more brightly, "but I think I could larn most things."

"Humph!" said Eli; then after a pause added, "Well, lad, thou'rt not fit to look for a job to-day, for the weather's pinching cold. So stay here an' keep warm, and to-morrow we'll have a talk. What's thy name?"

"Joe Bradley, sir."

"Joe what?"

"Bradley."

"Bah! I never knew a Bradley good for owt yet."

"P'r'aps you never know'd many of 'em," said Joe.

"I knew one, any road," said Eli; an' I never want to know another if they're all like him."

To this Joe made no reply; and Eli sat for a long time as if in deep thought, glancing every now and then across at Joe, as if trying to read some secret in his face. At length he asked abruptly, "Are thy father an' mother living?"

"I don't know—I hope so," said Joe, and then he proceeded to tell all his story, with which the reader is already acquainted.

Eli made no reply when Joe had finished; but his face wore an anxious and troubled expression, and Joe noticed that he went to his work again, leaving his dinner almost untasted.

He asked Joe no more questions that day. But next morning he astonished our hero with the question:

" Joe, would ye like to be a blacksmith ? "

" Aye, wouldn't I just ! " said Joe, with his face brightening.

" An' could yer put up living with a crusty old badger like me ? "

" What, in this grand 'ouse ? " said Joe, his eyes growing wide with wonder.

" Aye lad," said Eli with a laugh, amused at Joe calling his simple cottage-home a grand house; and yet to the poor homeless lad it seemed a palace. " Aye, lad, sleep here at nights, an' work in the shop during the day."

" But ye're only teasin'," said Joe, his face dropping. " It's too good for ye to mean it."

" Nay, lad," said Eli, " I'm in sober earnest." I want a strong boy, an' Providence has sent thee here. At least, it looks mighty like it."

Joe could make no further answer; his heart was too full. Hiding his face in the sofa he began to cry, for he was yet only weak, and unable to control his feelings.

Nor was Eli altogether unmoved, and once or twice he blew his nose in a very suspicious fashion. The story that Joe had told him—how he had fancied the ring of his anvil was the music of heaven, saying to him all the while, " Come home, come home "—had touched his heart in an unaccountable fashion.

Was it a mysterious Providence, he wondered, that led him to make nails that evening, and so, all unconsciously, to ring out a welcome to this poor starving lad ?

" An' *this* lad of all other lads," he said to himself.

" Ah me ! ah me ! Life is very wonderful, an' God's ways are past finding out."

As soon as Joe was strong enough, he set to work with a will ; and, oh ! what a delight it was, when the weather was pinching cold outside, to see the flames in the forge leap up, and hear the bellows roar ! While the first day on which he swung the big hammer he felt that he would never forget to his dying day. How the sparks flew around him like a golden shower as his blows fell heavy and thick on the red-hot iron, while the ring and rhythm of the two hammers—his and Eli's—made music as sweet as anything he had ever heard !

" That'll do," said Eli at length ; " and for the future, Joe, whenever I let my hammer dither on the anvil, instead of striking the iron, that'll be the signal for you to stop. Dost understand ? "

" Aye," said Joe, wiping the perspiration from his forehead, " I think I do."

" That's right. Now whistle a stave o' ' God save the Queen.' "

" Can't do that," said Joe, making a desperate effort, and failing.

" How's that ? " said Eli with a laugh.

" Ain't got no puff," said Joe.

Eli had no cause to regret employing Joe in the place of his runaway apprentice. The lad was strong, quick-witted, willing to be corrected, and eager to learn.

So the days sped away rapidly and soon glided into weeks, while Joe felt happier almost than he had ever felt before in his life. It was true he was still anxious about his mother——of his father he thought little ; and every day, and almost every hour of the day, he wondered if ever he should see Daisy again.

The first time he went to the village church he thought he had found her : a little girl sat just before him, with hair just exactly like Daisy's ; but when she turned her head he discovered his mistake, and, with a sigh, he settled back in his seat and tried to fix his attention on the preacher. He soon got interested, too. The sermon was on the good Providence of God. How He led His children in strange ways, and made what seemed evil things subservient to their good. How, when earthly friends failed, God stood by them and sanctified poverty and pain and loss to their spiritual and eternal well-being.

There were many big words Joe could not understand, but the main drift of the sermon was quite clear to him. Had God led him, he wondered ; and as he thought of his own strange life, it did not seem unlikely. And if God could see everything, how easy it would be, he thought, for God to so arrange matters that he and his mother and Daisy should meet again.

" I b'leeve the gent knowed as 'ow I were goin' to be there," Joe said to himself as he left the church, " an' so spoke jist straight to me. But lor ! if that little gal 'ad only been Daisy, wouldn't it ha' been scrumpshous ! "

Joe was so pleased with the morning-service that he went again in the evening, and after that became one of the vicar's most regular hearers. Nearly every Sabbath he heard something new ; and when the

As soon as Joe was strong enough, he set to work with a will.—*Page 173.*

sermon puzzled him, Eli generally helped him out of his difficulty during the week.

So Joe grew in mind and body, and in morals as well; and had any of his old acquaintances seen him six months after he came to Three Lanes End, dressed in a new suit of corduroy, they would scarcely have recognised him.

When summer came, Joe was in a seventh heaven of delight. For when the day's work was over, he could roam the lanes and fields at his own sweet will, and revel in summer's beauty to his heart's content.

There was one spot he visited nearly every day, and that—where, hungry, despairing, and almost frozen, he lay down to die. How different the place looked now in the summer warmth and sunshine. The tree—a sycamore—was now in full leaf, and high up among its branches a thrush poured forth its wealth of song nearly every evening. Here, if he was too tired for a ramble, he often came and sat himself down to read, or more often to dream, and wonder what the future would bring him.

As high up as he could reach, he had cut his initials, J. B., in the bark of the tree. This was his " Bethel " and his " Ebenezer " also. Here God had been with him, and here God had led him.

" Oh, if God would lead his mother here also ! " This was his daily thought and almost daily prayer.

" Be patient, Joe," Eli would say, if ever he talked to him about the matter. " God knows best."

Joe could not have fallen into kinder hands than Eli's. There was a touch of nature somewhere that

M

linked their hearts in genuine affection, and had they been father and son they could scarcely have loved each other more.

So time passed on, and summer faded into mellow autumn, and autumn gave place to winter, and winter bloomed into spring once more, when a circumstance transpired that must be recorded in another chapter.

CHAPTER X.

"COALS OF FIRE.

"I am weary, let me rest;
  Life will soon be o'er with me;
Death I welcome to my breast,
  Though, too, filled with mystery;
I have most unfaithful been,
  Have not tried to do my best,
For the good that might have been—
  I am tired—let me rest!"
                    —Florence Dudley.

IT was a biting cold day in March, with a keen east wind sweeping along the hillside that was far more trying to the sensibilities than the severest frost could have been. Joe had been across the fields to a neighbouring farm about some work that wanted doing, and was now returning at a swinging pace, stimulated to put on his best speed by the thought of supper, and by the admonitions of an ever-faithful appetite.

The best and least exposed way would have been round by the lane. But Joe was in a hurry to get home, and, as he didn't mind in the least the piping wind, he took a straight cut across the fields.

He was within a field of the smithy, when, on leaping over a hedge, he espied, not a gun-shot, away a ragged, forlorn-looking creature creeping along in the ditch, as if afraid of being observed. For several seconds Joe stood watching the wretched creature, much wondering who he could be or what he wanted, then marched boldly forward for the purpose of confronting him.

As soon as the lad—for he was only a lad— caught sight of Joe, he slunk suddenly back into the ditch, and tried to hide himself in the thick undergrowth.

"Come," said Joe, in his sternest manner; "ye needn't try to hide, so come out o' it."

"Oh, please, don't give me up!" cried the lad on finding himself discovered; "oh, don't! for Heaven's sake, don't!"

At the sound of his voice Joe started back as though some one had shot him. He felt certain that he knew the voice, though to whom it belonged, or where, or when, or under what circumstances he had heard it, he could not for the moment remember.

Seeing his hesitancy, the lad cried out again, "Oh, please, don't give me up; I'm nearly dead, I be for sure!"

"Come out here, then, an' let me look at yer,"

said Joe; and, without any more hesitancy, the lad obeyed.

One look into the face was sufficient. " Swivel ! " he cried out, with suppressed excitement, " an' so I've caught yer at last, 'ave I ? "

" Caught me ? " said Swivel, crouching in terror at his feet, " what yer mean ? "

" I mean what I say," said Joe, trembling all over; " an' the last time I looked into yer lying face, I vowed if ever I did catch yer again I'd pound yer to a jelly."

" What yer mean ? " said Swivel, " an' who be you?"

" So you've forgotten me, have yer ? " Joe replied; ' any road, I've not forgotten you."

" But who be you ? " Swivel persisted.

" I'm Joe Bradley," was the reply. " You 'member how you tried to make a thief o' me, and laughed at me when I were nabbed."

" No, no ! " said Swivel, drawing himself up and looking Joe straight in the face ; you're a-foolin' me."

" Do I look like it ? " Joe replied.

But Swivel made no answer. He was too astonished to speak, and Joe went on again. " Now what yer think you deserve ? I've a good mind "— and Joe doubled his fists, but did not finish the sentence.

" Oh, don't, please ; don't ! " cried Swivel, bursting into a violent fit of coughing. Then, after a while, he gasped, " I desarve anythink, but 'ave pity. I'm clemmed, an' ill, an' nearly dead ; I be for sure."

And as Joe looked into the pinched and haggard

face of the wretched lad, he felt that his words were
true, and his heart smote him with a sudden spasm
of pain. He remembered still that talk with the
chaplain about the duty of forgiveness, and the
blessedness of doing good, and felt that his treatment of Swivel came very far short of the chaplain's standard. It was a fierce battle he had to
fight with himself. At one moment his anger would
seem to gain the mastery. The next moment pity
and compassion would triumph, and he longed
to take the suffering lad in his arms and comfort
him.

"Swivel," he said at length, and his voice was
gentle and subdued, "you treated me real mean once,
but it's turned out well, an' I've learned a many
things in the last year; and now, instead of punchin
yer head, I'll forgive yer; an' if ye'll come into our
shop, I'll warm yer, and give yer a crust."

"And not give me up to the capt'in?" said Swivel
eagerly.

"Is it the captain that's after you?" Joe asked.

"Aye, he wants me back," Swivel answered, colour-
ing slightly.

"Swivel," said Joe, more in pity than in anger,
"you're sich a awful liar, that there's no b'leevin'
anything as you say. But let that go. I'll not give
yer up, so come with me."

It was much easier, however, for Joe to say " come '
than it was for Swivel to obey, and, finding that he
was scarcely able to walk, Joe took him on his back
and carried him into the smithy, and soon succeeded
in producing a cheerful fire (for Eli had left off work

and had gone into the house). Scarcely had Swivel begun to enjoy the genial warmth than he started up in affright.

"There they be," he hissed; "they're after me;" and before Joe knew what he meant, he had slipped off the forge, lifted the corner of a tool-chest, and slipped inside, letting the lid fall with a bang.

A moment or two later two men came up to the door, and, after a hurried glance round the shop, said in a careless fashion, "Cold day, this!"

"Aye," said Joe, "it's a sneezer."

"Yes, very cold. By the by, you've not seen a lad pass along either of these roads lately, have you?"

"Lor, what a question!" laughed Joe. "Why folks often passes along this way. But I ain't seen nobody pass 'ere lately, 'cause I've only just got back from Willow Farm."

"Oh, indeed!" and, with another suspicious glance round the smithy, they departed.

When they were well out of sight, Joe raised the corner of the tool-chest, and Swivel, half suffocated, struggled out, glad enough to escape from his confinement. At the same moment Eli came in to see what Joe was after, as he expressed it, and was soon made to understand the state of affairs.

"Humph!" said Eli. "An' so this is the very lad that nearly ruined thee, eh? That got thee sent to gaol, an' laughed at thy downfall. Humph! this is a strange world, an' things do come about mighty queer."

"But I didn't mean 'im to be nabbed," said Swivel, not at all relishing the drift of the conversation.

"Likely not," said Eli; "but Joe's got his turn, an' I'm glad he's making a right use o' it. Thou means to punish him well, Joe?"

"Nay, master," said Joe, "I've forgived 'im."

At these words Eli turned away his head to hide the moisture that suddenly gathered in his eyes; while poor Swivel was so completely overcome that he burst into tears, the first he had shed for many a day.

That night Swivel was stripped of his dirty rags and laid in Joe's clean bed, and next morning he was so ill that Joe had to fetch a doctor.

Poor Swivel never rallied. Hunger, exposure, and cold had done their work, and severe inflammation of the lungs cut short a neglected and misspent life.

"Joe," said Swivel, a few days before he died, "I dunnow 'ow yer could a done it."

"Done what, Swivel?" Joe asked.

"A took me in an' forgive me," Swivel answered, with the tears starting in his eyes.

"I scarce know myself," Joe said, after a pause. "But I'll tell yer all I knows: all that the chaplain an' Mr. Eli 'ave told me, an' all I've heard at church." And sitting down by the bedside, he told the dying lad all he knew of the wonderful Gospel story, and the infinite love of Christ. And as he warmed with his theme, words came to his lips in a way that he had never known the like of before.

Swivel listened with closed eyes and trembling lips.

There was evidently something in the " old, old story," told in childish language, that touched the heart of this poor erring lad to its very depths, and made him feel as he never had felt before.

" An' does yer mean to say, Joe," he said at length, " that God'll forgive anybody as is sorry, an' as axes Him."

" Aye," said Joe, " anybody. The very worst."

" Then, in that case," said Swivel, " I'll ax Him."

And there and then, for the first time in his life Swivel began to pray. We will not give his prayer, lest it should shock some fastidious soul by its seeming irreverence. But He who seeth not as man seeth, took no heed, we think, of the *form* of the prayer, but only of the desire which it expressed. This, at least, we *know*,—that after Swivel had prayed, he lay back in his bed comforted.

During all the weeks of his illness Joe nursed him as though he had been his own brother, never alluding to the past, nor even asking him what crime he had committed that the detectives were on his track. The wrong that Swivel had done him, God had changed to good. And he felt sometimes as though Swivel had been his friend, so strangely had God overruled all the events of his life and made them work together for his good.

Every time that Joe came into the room, the wan, pinched face of the dying lad would light up as though a ray of sunshine fell upon it ; and, taking Joe's horny hands in his own wasted palms, he would say, " Ye *are* good, Joe ; an' I'm very happy ! "

And truly he looked the picture of content. The

chastening hand of affliction had smoothed away the cunning and suspicion from his face, and into his eyes a look of tenderness had come, unknown in the old days. His bed was soft and clean, what he had not known since he could remember; and every day Joe brought fresh flowers into the room, and spoke to him of the better land, where the flowers would never fade.

" I don't want to get better," he would often say; " I'm so happy lyin' here."

And Joe would smooth his pillow and say nothing. His heart would often be too full for words. In some strange way he was getting to love the lad that once he hated; and as the day of Swivel's departure grew perceptibly nearer, he fretted as though he were losing his dearest friend.

" It's strange ye should cry for sich as me," Swivel said to him the day before he died. " I don't understand it all."

" Nor I either," Joe replied; " but it's a fact I do love yer very much; you ain't like you used to be, Swivel."

" Ain't I, Joe ? " Swivel answered with a smile. " I'm glad you think I'm betterin'; but I owes it all to you, Joe.

After this conversation he spoke very little, and on the following day he fell into a heavy sleep, from which he never woke, but gradually passed into the deeper sleep of death. Joe watched by his side until the last, hoping for one last look of recognition, but it was never given. One labouring sigh was heard, and then the heart grew still; and Joe knew that all was over. Pressing a hasty kiss on the still warm brow, he hurried out of the room, and went and sat under his favourite sycamore, and gave way to a flood of tears.

CHAPTER XI.

A SUFFICIENT ANSWER.

"Like presentiment of danger,
 Though the sky no shadow flings;
Or that inner sense, still us anger,
 Of unseen, unuttered things."
 —SWAIN.

AFTER the death of Swivel life went on at the smithy just as before, and with little of change to mark the passing days. Joe was more contented with his lot than he had ever been before in his life. He liked his work; he liked his home; he liked his master; while the surrounding country was beautiful at all seasons of the year, and he had plenty of leisure to ramble over hill or dale whenever he felt the inclination to do so.

Nor was that all. He had learnt to read—Eli declared—like a parson, and began to appreciate the companionship of books, while Eli helped him in every possible way.

He had never been treated as a servant, nor even as an apprentice. Indeed, had he been the old man's own child he could not have had more forbearance shown him. Why was this?

This was a question that perplexed Joe nearly every day of his life. Of course he knew very well that he was not dependent on the old man's charity. He was earning all he got, and perhaps a little bit more; for Joe took to the hammer and anvil, as Eli said, "like a duck takes to water." Indeed, the lad had quite a genius in some directions, and was soon able to fashion delicate bits of work with almost as much skill as Eli himself. Yet this of itself, Joe felt, was not sufficient to explain the old man's uniform kindness and consideration.

So time went on, and Joe seemed to get no nearer a solution of the problem. Once in a while Eli would ask him some question relative to his past life, but in such an off-hand manner as to indicate that he felt no special interest in the matter. And once, and only once, he had asked him what he would do if his parents should turn up again. Would he forsake the smithy, and go on the tramp once more?

This question considerably perplexed Joe. He hated the gipsy life he had led in the old days, and yet he dearly loved his mother, and sometimes he felt that if she ever appeared on the scene again he would leave all and follow her.

So the days passed on, and spring bloomed into beautiful summer once more, and every day Joe kept a sharp look-out along the roads that converged at Three Lanes End, in the hope that his parents might pass that way; and the more he thought about the matter, the stronger grew his desire to see his mother. Indeed, it became a positive hunger after a while, and threatened seriously to affect his spirits and his health.

He felt certain that they must pass Three Lanes End sooner or later, for they visited every village in the country; his only fear being that they might pass it when he was not on the look-out.

Eli knew of his anxiety, and so assisted in the watch; and as the smithy commanded a long stretch of two out of the three roads, this was not difficult. At meal-times Joe sat with his face to the window, so that no one passed without his seeing him or her, as the case might be. And scarcely a footfall sounded in the night-time that Joe did not hear, and rush to the window to see whose it might be.

In those days his mother filled all his thoughts. As for Daisy, she was gradually fading from his memory like a pleasant dream.

Sometimes he was half disposed to think he had dreamed it all: that Daisy had no real existence, or that, if she had, it was in a fairer world than this. Perhaps God had given him a vision of one of His angels, just to encourage him in his struggle towards the better life, and that only in that home which she was the first to speak to him about would he find her again.

As summer ripened into autumn, and young and old

in the cornfields made merry in the sunshine, Joe grew more and more restless and ill at ease.

During the first year of his separation from his parents he gave up expecting their return, and submitted to the inevitable with a cheerfulness that was surprising. But as time wore on he began to expect their return, and the expectation increased his longing, and intensified his hunger for a sight of his mother's face.

One day, early in September, he was seated at table with Eli, eating his dinner. The meal did not proceed very rapidly, for a difficult piece of work was under discussion, and each had an opinion to express on the matter, when suddenly, in the middle of a sentence, Joe ceased speaking, dropped his knife and fork on his plate with a clatter, and commenced to stare out of the window as though he had suddenly been bereft of his senses.

" Well, Joe, what is it ? " said Eli.

But Joe paid no heed to the old man's question, but continued to stare at some object coming along the road. Then, suddenly crying out, " Glory ! it's my mother ! " he overturned his chair, and nearly the table, and rushed to the door with all possible haste.

True enough, it was his mother ; but for a moment she scarcely recognised him, so much was he changed.

" Why, mother, don't you know me ? " Joe cried, pressing her hands. "I'm Joe, yer own boy Joe."

In a moment the bundle of canes fell from her shoulders, and Joe was in her arms. She could not speak, but hot tears of joy fell upon his face, while she kissed him again and again. Then, holding him at arm's length, she looked eagerly into his face, as if fearful she had made a mistake.

" My blessed boy ! " she cried ; " an' is it really you ? Oh, Joe, my heart will break wi' joy ! " and back to her bosom she pressed him again, and covered his face with kisses.

By this time Eli had appeared on the scene, with eyes that looked very suspicious of tears. For a moment Joe's mother did not notice him. When she caught sight of him, however, she started back as though something had stung her, and seemed almost ready to fall.

" Is it possible ? " she gasped at length, with blanched lips. " Is it "——

" Yes, Ruth," Eli said in a broken voice ; " it is thy father."

But she did not go near him ; she only slunk farther away, keeping tight hold of Joe all the while.

" Ah, you shrink from me still ! " he said. " But no wonder. I vowed if ever you married Bradley you should never darken my door again or be a child of mine. But God has changed my heart since then, and shown me the folly of trying to defy Nature's law. Ruth, thou'rt my child still ; wilt come to thy father ? "

She needed no second bidding, and a moment later father and child were locked in a long embrace, and in that moment of joy all the past was forgotten.

But what need is there that we should further describe the scene ? No more work was done in the smithy that day, and in the evening Eli chopped his daughter's bundles of canes into " kindlin'," as he called it, though they proved to be anything but a success in that direction.

"God has sent thee home, Ruth, in thy widowhood," he said; "and God sent thy boy here before thee. I knew he was thine from the first, and I have loved him for thy sake, as well as his own. Thou hast had enough of wandering, and Joe and I need thee here; and here thou shalt stay to keep house for us, an' this shall be thy home."

And for answer she kissed him, her heart being too full for words. But the answer was sufficient for both Eli and Joe.

CHAPTER XII.

AT LAST.

" Hand-in-hand o'er the rugged strand
  Of life we are journeying on ;
  And patiently wait till the pearly gate
  Is reached, and the crown is won."
  —FLORENCE DUDLEY.

FIVE years passed away, transforming Joe from a
big awkward lad into a tall, well-knit young
man. Upon Eli's head the years fell lightly,
for he looked scarcely any older than when we first
saw him ; but over Ruth Bradley's head they seemed
to have flown with healing in their wings, for not
only did she look no older, but everybody declared
that she looked five years younger. The weary look
of anxiety and care had passed away from her face
completely, and in its place had come an expression of
peace and content. After a heart-breaking search of
nearly two years, she had found her boy again, and
now, for five peaceful years, she had had a settled
home, without once feeling the pinch of poverty or
the pain of neglect. It was no wonder she looked
younger. Her married life had been a sad one from
first to last. She had run away from home to marry

her husband,—an idle, loafing, discontented man; for twelve years she had tramped the country with him, living a weary hand-to-mouth existence. It was no wonder she looked old before her time, and a few more such years would have laid her in the grave.

It would be difficult to say which was the more proud of Joe,—his mother or his grandfather. Eli spoke of " Our Joe," as he always called him, as if he were quite a genius; and Ruth spoke of " Our Joe " as if he were the best son that ever gladdened a mother's heart. Nor were they proud of him without reason. He was as true as the steel he welded, and as firm in his honesty as the anvil that echoed to the stroke of his hammer. That he was skilful at his trade also there could be no doubt; and so much had the business increased, that the smithy had to be enlarged, and the staff had been increased by one journeyman and two apprentices; so that Joe and Eli were now looked upon as fairly prosperous men.

During all these years Joe had never seen Daisy, or had been able to get any clue whatever as to her whereabouts. He often wondered what had become of her, for to forget her wholly was out of the question. He always felt that Daisy was the first to start him on the road towards the better life; from her lips he got his first definite idea of heaven, the better land.

Now and then he had had his dreams: that he should yet find her in trouble or in danger, and with his strong arm he should come to her rescue, and so repay in some measure the kindness she had shown him in the darkest days of his life. But his dreams

never came to anything, and he did not suppose that
if they met now they would recognise each other.
" If he had grown into a man, she must be nearly a
woman ; " such was his thought.   What hope, therefore,
had he of ever finding his little friend ?   So five
years passed away, as we have already stated, when
new tenants came to Willow Farm.   This was a
matter of some interest to Eli and Joe, as the change
made it somewhat uncertain as to whether they would
still be favoured with the work of the farm.   On the
Sunday Joe looked out for the new farmer and his
family at church, but they did not put in an appearance ; and during the week he learned that they had
taken a pew in the village chapel.   Hence two or
three weeks passed away ere he could get a peep at
the " new people," and so have his curiosity on that
point gratified.

And to get his " peep," we may as well confess it,
Joe paid a visit to the chapel in question, and was placed
in a pew on a line with the one occupied by the farmer.
Joe was there early, and so saw Farmer Rimmer,
followed by his two daughters and three sons, enter the
chapel and walk up through the aisle.   And yet Joe saw
only one face, and that the face of the eldest daughter,
and for several minutes after the family was seated
he kept his eyes fixed in the same direction.   What
was it in that face that attracted him so ?   For his
life he could not tell.   He did not know that this
tall, sweet-faced maiden was his old friend Daisy.
How should he ?   And yet such was the case.   He
supposed that she was Miss Rimmer; the thought
that she might be Daisy Blake never once crossed his

mind. He had quite given up the hope of meeting her again; and so he sat all through the service, hearing nothing of the singing or the sermon, but puzzling himself hopelessly over the problem of this girl's face.

As they were leaving, at the close of the service, they met face to face in the aisle. For a moment Daisy started as she encountered the steady gaze of the tall young man before her; but no look of recognition came into her eyes, and, turning her head quickly, she walked with rapid steps out of the chapel.

Joe puzzled himself through a great part of the night, and through most of the following week, but with no satisfactory result. Then, rating himself roundly for his folly, he tried to think no more about the matter. But that he found to be an impossiblity. Try as he would, Daisy's sweet face haunted him almost night and day. So matters went on for a fortnight, when Joe discovered that the young lady in question was Farmer Rimmer's niece, and not his daughter, as he had always believed. In a moment the thought struck him, " Can she be Daisy ? "

Off Joe started as soon as his work was done in the evening for Willow Farm. The sun was still above the horizon, and in the fields the hay-makers were still busy at their work, while, from numberless hedges and trees, the birds were flooding all the air with song. But Joe had neither eye nor ear for anything to-day. All his thought was of Daisy. In a field near the farm-house two girls were milking, and for several minutes Joe stopped outside the hedge watching them. " Yes, that's her," he said to himself at length ; " the one I saw in the chapel. though she

doesn't look quite the same with that sun-bonnet on
and her sleeves tucked up to her elbows."

At length he turned away with a sigh, and began
to retrace his steps. " She may be the farmer's
niece," he said, " but she ain't Daisy; so it's no use
bothering any longer."

He did bother himself, nevertheless, and often,
through the dewy fields, in the quiet eventide, he
sauntered in the direction of Willow Farm, sometimes
going through the farm-yard, and beyond it, and then
back again.

It was strange how the memory of Daisy, once
aroused from its long slumber, haunted him. For
years she had been to him only as a dream; now the
old desire to find her came back with tenfold power.

" I've never half searched for her," he said to himself. " These folks came here from Lowerdyke, not
three miles away, and yet I never heard of their
existence till they came to Willow Farm. As like as
not Daisy's somewhere in the neighbourhood. I'll
begin again, and make a proper search."

These thoughts were passing through his mind one
evening as he sat on a stile whittling a stick, and so
absorbed was he that he did not notice Daisy's approach
until she came close up to him.

In a moment he jumped off the stile for her to
pass. " By Jupiter! I b'leeve she's Daisy, after all,"
was the thought that darted through his mind like a
lightning flash.

" Beg your pardon, miss," he said suddenly, " but
may I ask if your name is Daisy Blake?"

" Yes," she answered, a little bit scornfully he

thought; "that is my name. Did you want anything?"

Joe hung his head for a moment, while a hot flush passed over his face. "Wanted anything?" The question seemed to him almost an insult, and from *her* lips too.

"I beg pardon," he stammered; "I think you don't know me."

"Oh, yes, I do," she answered quickly. She meant that she knew him as the blacksmith of Three Lanes End; but he misunderstood her, and his face crimsoned to the roots of his hair. Such a "cut" he had never expected to get.

"I'm sorry I spoke," he said, in a low tone of voice, and turned and marched swiftly away.

For some time Daisy stood watching him, wondering who he reminded her of, and what he could mean by asking her such a question. His face had perplexed her when she met him in the chapel that Sunday evening. Now she was perplexed more than ever. There was something, too, in the tone of his voice that reminded her of something long forgotten, and awoke memories of other days and years far back in the past. But she was very far from guessing the truth. She had often thought of the poor lad that had befriended her in her greatest trouble; often wished that she might see him again; often wondered what he had thought when she never returned to him in Angel's Court, according to promise. But she had long since given up hope of meeting him again.

Poor Joe, half angry, half sad, returned to Three Lanes End, and moped all the rest of the evening.

To think that Daisy should confess that she knew
him, and yet treat him as she had done, was as worm-
wood and gall to him.   He had found her at last, but
the discovery had only brought him pain.

"Proud thing!" he said to himself; "but I'll never
trouble her again;" and he kept his vow.

It was nearly a month after when they met again
and then Daisy came to the smithy to get a corn-
hook mended, and waited for it to be done.   Joe was
very quiet, and barely civil, while Daisy looked at
him, puzzled both by his face and manner.

When the hook was mended, Joe handed it to her
her without a word.

"What have I to pay for it, please?" she asked.

"Nothing," Joe answered abruptly.

"Nothing!" she said, in some surprise.

"Nothing to you, Miss Blake," Joe answered, in
gentler tones.   "You were kind to me once, and
helped me when I was in sore need.   If I can show
a kindness to you in any way, I shall only be too
happy."

"I do not understand," Daisy said, looking bewildered.

"You said, when last we met, that you knew me,"
Joe replied.

"Of course I knew you were the blacksmith," she
answered.

"But not as the boy you knew in Angel's Court?"
Joe asked.

"What!" she cried, looking more astonished than
ever.   "Are you really Joe—Joe Bradley?"

"I'm the very same," Joe answered.

Joe showed Daisy the tree.—Page 203.

" Oh, I am glad to see you ! " she replied, her face brightening. " I had given up hope of ever seeing you again. Now I understand how your face and voice have puzzled me so."

" Shall I walk home with you ? " Joe asked, a little dubiously.

" I shall be so glad if you will," was the answer ; " I've so many things to tell you, and so many questions to ask."

So they walked away together, through the quiet fields, in the slanting evening light, Joe carrying the hook ; and when they reached the farm-house, they had not told each other half they wanted to tell.

How the memory of old times came back, with all the pain and squalor of Angel's Court !

" How strange," said Daisy, as they were about to say good-night, " that we should have lived for seven years or more, within less than three miles of each other, and never recognised each other till now ! "

"Aye, 'tis strange," said Joe ; and the more he thought of it, the stranger it seemed.

Daisy and Joe often met after that, for they had much to tell each other ; and when he went to Willow Farm, Farmer Rimmer always gave him a hearty welcome.

Joe showed Daisy the tree under which he lay himself down to die, that winter night, and the letters he had since cut in its bark in memory of the goodness of God. Indeed, he told her all his story from the time he watched her tripping down Angel's Court, that dreary November day, till the time they met again more than seven years after.

Daisy had little to tell. She had been very happy with her uncle and aunt and cousins, and the years had glided very peacefully away, with very little of interest to mark their flight.

"But I can't tell you how pleased I am, Joe, to find you again," she said; "and to find you what you are."

"You were the first, Daisy," he answered, "to set me on the track towards the better life. And a good deal of what I am I owe to you."

.   .   .   .   .

Several years have passed away since that meeting. Joe is a master smith to-day (for Eli has retired from the business). Steadily his business increases, and he is making a comfortable income. But, what is better still, he is known in the neighbourhood as a man of sterling honesty and of true Christian character.

Ruth Bradley still keeps house for her father, and Eli declares "that his last days are his best."

Across the way a new house has been built, larger and more pretentious than the cottage that adjoins the shop, and filled with more elaborate furniture. While it was building many people wondered who it could be for. But that speculation has been set at rest long since. And nobody is surprised now-a-days when Daisy also, as well as Eli and Ruth, speak of the hero of this little story as

"OUR JOE."

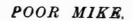

POOR MIKE.

CHAPTER I.

EARLY DAYS.

"YES, thankee, I'm doin' bravely now, and 'll soon be as right as ninepence again, I'm thinkin'."

The speaker was a lad of some thirteen or fourteen years of age. He might have been fifteen; it was hard to tell. When his face was in repose, and his thoughts were wandering back over the past, he looked almost *old ;* but when he was engaged in conversation his face would brighten, and his eyes would shine like twin-stars, while the careworn and aged expression would vanish as if by magic, and there would beam upon you a bright boyish face, that might never have been touched by the hand of care or grief.

"She said as how you were comin'," he went on, with a jerk of his thumb in the direction of a lady who was talking to a visitor in another part of the large room; "so I've been expectin' on ye. You ain't owt like I'd thought you'd be, though."

"Indeed!"

"No, not a bit; but that don't matter, I'm thinkin': but I've been wantin' to see yer bad."

" Have you ? "

" Aye, to be sure ; ever sin' I read about that little chap yer tells about in the book."

" What little chap is that ? "

" Why, Benny—'Her Benny,' as the little gal used to call 'im. My, weren't he a stunner ? I larfed fit to kill mysel' when he got stuck in the mud ; you remembers, don't you ? "

" Oh, yes, quite well."

" Aye, of course you do ! I'd liked to have seen 'im an' little Nell, though. Pity she kicked the beam in that way, weren't it ? I greeted awful 'bout that, but p'r'aps 't were all for the best. She says," with another jerk of the thumb in the direction of the lady already spoken of, " that everythin' 's for the best : I hope it are, but things look mighty crooked sometimes."

And for a moment or two the old careworn look settled upon his face, and his eyes caught a wistful far-away expression that was almost pitiful to see.

" You never heard 'bout my little sister, very likely," he went on after a pause. " She weren't as big as Nelly. Would you like to hear 'bout her ? "

" Very much."

" Oh ! then I'd better begin at the beginnin' :— Years an' years ago we used to live in the country, that is, father an' mother an' me. May weren't born then, and all the others died when they were babies. I don't remember nothin' 'bout them very much, but that don't matter ; they're better off, I reckon, than those who live to get older. Father used to make shoes. I mind his little shop very well at the end of the 'ouse, with it's slantin' roof. I used to climb up it sometimes when father was not about, an' then slide right off. It weren't far to drop, an' the turf was soft, and I know I was mighty fond of climbin' in those days. I've 'ud plenty since of another sort.

" Well, as I was a-saying, father used to make shoes. There weren't many houses round about; so father only had work enough to keep him at home three days a week; the other three days he used to work for old Naylor in the village, two miles away, or maybe more.

" Mother liked father to be home best, for then she could sit with him sometimes an' do her sewin'. An' I know she lik'd that, for she used to smile so glad-like and look so happy. *I* didn't mind much anyway, for you see, when father was out of the way I could do a bit of slidin' on the roof on my own account; though I liked him to be home, too, for he was rare good company, and used to tell some stunnin' good stories.

" I don't think father was ever very strong, an' durin' the winter he used to have a desp'rate bad cough sometimes. I used to like him to be home in the winter, when it were wet an' cold, for then we used to have a jolly good fire in the shop, and I would be stoker. An' didn't I make a rare stoker, that's all ! You may bet I never let the fire go out when I had it in hand.

" Not very far away from our house was a big wood. Don't I mind that wood, though ? It *were* a wood, were that ! I've never seen owt like it

O

anywhere else! I got nearly lost in it once or twice, an' thought I'd never get out again, it were that big. An' didn't the wind roar in it on stormy days an' nights, that's all? Oh my! you should a-heard it, or you can 'ave no hidea.

"It all comes back to me now sometimes when I cannot sleep, and I hear the wind a-roarin' and a-sighin' as I used to do when a little chap at home.

"I mind now as how I used to like the wind to be high; I've felt different since, but no matter; I think of it now, how on stormy nights I used to lie awake an' listen to the wind roarin' in the wood. Sometimes it would go quiet for a minute or two, an' everything would be so silent that I could hear the old clock tickin' at the top of the stairs; then it would begin again—just a whisper at first, then it 'ud burst out all of a sudden, as though 't were in a terrible rage, an' I could hear the trees a-tossin' their arms about, an' the leaves a-rustlin' agin each other. It were grand music, too. Have you ever 'eard the wind like that?"

"Yes, many times."

"An' kept awake to listen to it?"

"Yes."

"Then you've lived in the country, maybe?"

We nodded assent.

"Ah, then you'll know all 'bout it. But I'm not gettin' on very fast with my story. I was goin' to tell yer how we was allowed to gather sticks in that wood that I was speakin' to you of. An' after a good stormy night in the autumn or winter, you may guess there 'ud be some store of sticks.

" Sometimes, after lyin' 'wake for a long time in the night listenin' to the wind, I'd be sleepin' late in the mornin', an' father 'ud come to the foot of the stairs an' shout, ' Mike ! Mike ! we must be off to the wood at once, for there's been a rare storm durin' the night.'

" ' All right,' I'd say, jumpin' up, ' I'll be down in a minute ; ' for I was as proud as anythink for the dad to ax me to go with him. Of course I couldn't carry many sticks, but I was kind of company for him, an' could help him to get the sticks in a heap, you see.

" Sometimes we'd spend most of the day in bringin' home the fuel, and by evenin' we'd have a rare heap piled up in a corner of the shop. I used to like that, you may depend, for, you see, I could always be better stoker when there was plenty of fuel to work at.

" We'd have gran' times on winter evenin's, I can tell yer, when the wind was a-howlin' an' the snow comin' down. Father and mother 'ud be stitchin' away, an' I'd be keepin' the fire a-goin'. I used to like to watch their faces with the light of the fire fallin' on 'em, an' listen the while to the crackin' of the sticks, and the flames a-roarin' up the chimbley.

" Mother was always happier at sich times than when father was at the village ; it was easy to tell that by the look on her face. She'd a bonny face, too ; I've never seen a bonnier yet, though she lost all her roses afore she went. But, as I was a-sayin', she was never so happy as when the dad was workin at home. He never went to the village to work on a Saturday but somehow she got anxious and fidgety as evenin' came on. But as soon as ever she heard his footstep—an' she could tell it among a hundr'd—her face 'ud light up in a jiffy, an' she'd begin to sing as 'appy as a bird.

" But he was late sometimes, especially in winter, when the nights were dark an' cold. Then mother 'ud look anxious an' troubled like. She wouldn't say anythink to me. I was too little, I s'pose, or p'r'aps she didn't want me to know; but I know'd all the same, for I didn't hear her singin' downstairs, as she did on other nights.

" One night I mind very well wakin' up, an' hearin' nobody about, I called out for mother, and when she didn't speak I got frightened and called louder nor ever, but 't were no use; then I got out of bed and went downstairs, but she weren't to be seen anywhere. The candle was burnin' on the table, and the kettle singin' away by the fire as cheerful as anythink; but where mother was I couldn't make out, an' when I tried to open the door I found that it was locked an' the key gone.

" I mind very well beginnin' to cry, for I were dreadfully frightened, when I heard footsteps outside, and then I heard father's voice angry like, an' the next minute the key was put in the door, an' I slipped upstairs an' into bed in a jiffy. I didn't know then what it was that made father scold so, and use bad words, and be angry with mother, who was always so good. I've found out since.

" Next mornin' father was downright ill, an' as

cross an' miserable as he could be, an' mother seemed very partickler not to vex him, though nothin' seemed to please him very much. He didn't even look at the newspaper for the day, an' that were a very rare thing for him, for he nearly always spent Sunday mornin' in readin' the paper. I don't know why he never would go to church or chapel: mother often used to ax him, but he never would go. But then he never did any work on the Sunday, so he wasn't a bad man.

"I used to wish he would go to church with mother an' me, but wishin' didn't mend it. He liked for us to go; and when I got a little bigger would go up with me to the very door of the Sunday school, but he'd never go in.

"I mind goin' to a day-school, too, for a little bit, 't weren't for very long; but lor'! we had some rare times while it lasted. Didn't I get a bumper once, though? I mind it as if 't were only yesterday. I was sittin' on a high form, swingin' my feet a foot off the floor, when I took to noddin', for it were precious hot weather, I mind, an' I was awful sleepy. The other boys were a-titterin', I was told after, to see me a-noddin' farther and farther. At last away I goes, with a reg'lar lurch, hittin' the floor a thunderin' rattle with my forehead, which fetched up the school-master with a start, an' made me see more stars than ever I saw afore or since.

"Didn't I look silly, though, when I picked myself up? an' didn't the other boys larf? Larf! why, they went into convulsive fits of apple-plexy, every one on 'em. You should ha' seen 'em twistin' about, an' holdin' their stomachs wi' both hands, an' tryin' to keep their faces straight for fear o' vexin' the master. One lad rolled right off the form, an' lay kickin' as if he'd got the 'spavins;' an' I believe he were bad for a week after, tryin' so hard to keep it in.

"You may bet I never went to sleep on a form after that, for, you see, I got a hidin' from the master into the bargain. But I reckon it's mighty hard for a lad to keep out of scrapes. Don't you think so?"

"Well, certainly, Mike, facts seem to point in that direction," we answered.

"Aye, jist so; but I reckon I'll not finish all my story to-day, an' I've not said a word 'bout little May yet. But you'll be comin' again, an' then I'll tell you some more, if you care to hear it."

CHAPTER II.

CHANGES.

GOOD - morning, Mike, and how are you to-day ? "

" Oh, I'm as bright as a button, thankee, an' as fresh as a daisy. Did I tell you I was gettin' new understandin' ? So I'll be standin' on a different footing soon altogether, and then shan't I cut a figure ? "

This was a grim, and painful joke, as the reader will understand by and by. But Mike Barlow was not one of those who go half-way to meet trouble ; he took things as they came with a cheerful spirit, and if he couldn't mend them he rarely complained.

" What's the use of worritin' ? " he said to me one day, " 't won't make things any better, and I believe in bein' cheerful; an' if I can't be 'appy like some folks, I ain't a-goin' to be miserable like others as I knows on."

So Mike philosophized in his own way, and, as the old hymn says,

"Put a cheerful courage on."

He was wonderfully bright and even humorous to-day, but soon settled into the serious business of telling his story; his manner evidently showing that he had been gathering up and arranging what facts he could remember since our previous meeting.

"I was a-tellin' you last time you was here," he went on, "as how I didn't stay long at the day-school; more's the pity, I'm thinkin', but that can't be helped now. You see, the beginnin' of it was, old Naylor died, an' another chap from Oldham or somewheres took the business, and put in a great winder in the shop, an' got in a sight of ready-made boots and shoes an' shined 'em up, an' made 'em look purty, to catch the eye of the village folk. An' then, after a bit, the young people turned up ther noses at home-made shoes—said as how they were clumsy, and not genteel, an' all that sort of thing; an' so, you see, father lost all the work he had at the village, an' had to depend on what he could git at home.

"Well, that were the beginnin' on it, you see. I don't think mother was sorry, for some things, for father had got into the habit lately of stayin' out rather late on a Saturday night, 'specially when the nights were cold. You see, the dad always liked a good fire, and was fond of a bit of company too; workin' so much alone p'r'aps made him more so.

Well, at the ' Blue Sheep ' there was a famous kitchen, an' a roarin' big fire on cold evenin's ; an' when father had finished his week's work he used to call in to have a glass to warm him for the journey home.

" Don't you go a-thinkin', however, that father was a drunkard. It was only on Saturday nights that he touched anythink at all, an' lots of times I've heard him say he only meant to stay a minute or so. But, you see, there 'd a'most sure to be somebody in the kitchen he know'd, who would ax the dad 'bout somethin' that were in the newspaper—for father was great on the newspaper ; he always got the *News of the World* or some'at of the sort every week, an' I don't believe he sca'ce missed a word of it from beginnin' to th' end.

" Well, as I was a-sayin', somebody 'ud ax him 'bout the news, or start a bit of a discussion or argyment, don't you see ? an' then time 'ud slip away 'mazin' quick, an', ye see, they'd be a-sippin' an' smokin' all the time ; and by the time the dad got up to go, why, he had more'n was good for him sometimes.

" That's how it comed about often and often, an' I know mother used to worrit 'bout it ; but she were never cross wi' him, but she used to tell him on a Saturday mornin' if he'd come home early she'd have a rare fire for him, an' a ham rasher for his supper. An' sometimes he would come home, and then you should ha' seen mother's face. Weren't it a picture, that's all !

" An' father 'ud say, ' There's no place like home, lass, after all.'

" An' then she'd smile all over her face like a basket of chips, and say she was glad he was pleased.

" ' Aye, lass,' he'd say, ' thee'rt a good wife, an' this ham is famous.'

" An' then she'd look as proud as a peacock, an' as pleased as anythink.

" I always liked for father to come home early on a Saturday night, for it made mother look so happy. So, you see, when old Naylor died, an' father had no more work at the village, mother thought maybe that he'd stay at home altogether. I don't think matters mended much, though, in that line.

" You see, when folks took so much to ready-made shoes, father had to depend mostly on mendin', an' that didn't pay as well as makin' new ones, an' he didn't like the work as well either : an' besides, when the jobs didn't come in fast enough he had to call on folks an' ax for their mendin', an' that he never could abide somehow, an' so I had to do that part of it after a bit, and sometimes mother. But mother 'ud do anythink to keep father home an' make him happy.

" So I was took away from school to help in gettin' bread, an' times got worse wi' us all the while. Little Sam was born 'bout that time too, I mind ; but he only lived a week or two, an' I reckon 't was best he died.

" I 'members very well the last day I were at school. We was just leavin' in the evenin' when a pack of hounds went yelpin' past, an' a fine sight of gentlemen in red coats a-gallopin' behind. Away they went right past the school-yard, over a gate, smashing it to shivereens, and down across the field like mad ; an' a lot of us boys took after 'em as fast as we could go. Didn't we run, that's all ! You should ha' seen us scramblin' over the hedges and across the ditches, and through the brakes of bracken an' all that sort of thing. We did raise a noise, you may depend.

"Well, after an hour or so, or maybe more, I got left all in the lurch, for I was only a little chap, eight or nine or so. Well, I struggled on till I couldn't go no farther, I was that done-up ; an', worse than any-think, I didn't no more know where I was than Jonah ; so, after I'd rested a bit, I climbed up a tree to 'ave a look around. It weren't a very big tree, which maybe was a good job. Anyhow, I comed down considerable faster than I went up. I don't know how it comed about ; but I'd nearly reached the top when something slipped, and away I comed with a whiz. I must ha' travelled purty fast, for seemed to me I'd no sooner got a-goin' than I stopped again. But the most curious part of it was, the ground seemed to come up to meet me ; and when we embraced, I tell you it was sudden an' onexpected like.

"I didn't 'member anythink after that for some time ; but when I was comin' a bit round I mind sayin' to myself very well,—

" ' Well, here I be, dead ! An' nobody 'll never find me ; an' I'll never be buried, an' nobody 'll never go to my funeral.'

"When I was a bit better I kept hollerin' an' shoutin' as loud as ever I could, an' after a bit a man found me, and then I 'members nothin' till next day, when I found myself in bed as stiff in my limbs as a tree an' as weak as a water-hen. I didn't go to school no more after that, and I didn't climb no more trees, though I've had climbin' enough since, but of another sort.

"Well, as I was a-sayin,' times got worse an' worse,

an' then, to finish up matters as were bad enough
before, a new railway was opened up right through
the village, an' cheap trips were run to Manchester on
market-days, an big shopkeepers put out bills all over
the place, that things could be had a'most for nothink
at their shops, an' great long pieces in the papers a-
statin' how they didn't want no profits, or next to
none.   Oh, dear, no !   They lived an' kept their big
shops open for the good of the public, an' all that sort
of thing.

" I've got to think since, that country-folks b'lieve
that kind of blarney a great deal more than folks who
lives in the towns do.   Anyhow, folks all round us
believed it, and lots of little shops were shut up
altogether.   I know father was awful mad about it,
an' used to say there weren't a chance for a poor man
who wanted to get an honest livin' ; an' mother used to
get very down-hearted too, sometimes, for the little
bit of money they saved all went durin' the bad times,
an' work got scarcer and scarcer, till times got that
bad that we was bound to shift.

" I mind it very well, an' thought 't was a gran'
thing to go to live in a great city like Manchester ;
I couldn't make it out no road why mother kept
greetin' all the while, an' why she was so down in the
dumps 'bout it.   Father didn't say very much, but I
think he fretted a bit too, for don't 'e see they'd lived
in the little cottage ever sin' they were wed, an' 't
was more like home to 'em than any other place could
ever be.

" I never told you 'bout the garden we had, did I ?
Well, it were a sight to see in the summer, a reg'lar

brake of flowers—an' the smell of 'em! Oh, dear! oh, dear! I couldn't describe it no road. An' mother were mighty fond of flowers, that she were, an' I guess she know'd she'd get no flowers in the city.

" It were a dismal day enough when we left the cottage : mother never stopped cryin' from mornin' till night. But I were in great spirits all the same. I'd heard so many stories 'bout the wonders of Manchester that I felt as light as a bird at the thought of goin'. Oh, dear! oh, dear! I didn't know what was comin', or I'd a-cried my heart out there and then.

" Father had taken a little house in a narrow street off Oldham Road. Oh, dear! how can I talk about it? All the splender of the city went away in a moment, an' never come back no more. My heart seem'd to drop into my shoes all of a sudden. Was that the grand house I had pictured an' dreamed about? That the grand street wi' gentlemen an' ladies passin' up an' down? But if we could only ha' kept at that it wouldn't ha' been so bad; but that was only the beginnin'.

" I cried myself to sleep that night, an' for many a night after; an' afore I'd been in the city a week I'd wished myself back in the old home a thousan' times. I was for long enough 'fore I could get used to the dirty women an' the ragged children in the street; but there was no help for it, so I had to put the best face on it I were able.

" Father got work at some big place in Oldham Street, but he didn't stay there long. They told him he were country-bred, an' didn't understand the city work ; an' for several days he were on the tramp afore he could get another place, an' then the work weren't reg'lar, an' sometimes for days an' days he had nothin' to do.

" Mother took in sewin' to help a bit, an' I picked up a copper or two now an' then goin' on errands. But, you see, I weren't used to city ways, an' there were heaps of little chaps quicker 'n me, so I stood a precious poor chance of makin' anythink out. Very likely if I'd lived in the city all my life I'd ha' managed better.

" The Lord knows we tried hard enough, every one of us, but the world seemed agin us, an' mother lost her roses an' father his temper, an' home like we used to 'ave we never had no more. When rent-day came we had to pawn some of the furniture to meet it. So one thing after another went, till in a year or so there was little left but bare walls.

" Poor mother ! she couldn't tell the dad now that if he'd come home early she'd have a great fire for him, an' a ham rasher for his supper ; an' so he didn't often come home early, an' mother never used to sing.

" I mind hearin' her say to him one day, ' I wish, Jack, you'd spend a evenin' at home with me sometimes, like you used to do.'

" ' Things ain't like they used to be,' he said. ' There's no comfort in a place like this ; an' when a fellow's been workin' in a stuffy cellar all day, he needs a bit of comfort, an' a drop to raise his spirits.'

" Mother didn't say nothin' in answer ; she only sighed an' turned away her head ; but I seen her cryin' afterwards, an' I know'd her heart was breakin'."

CHAPTER III

EVIL COMPANY.

" DID you ever think about a thing, an' think about it, an' greet over it, an' think about it again, till it got to be like a piece of yourself, and were always with you by night an' by day, when yer wakin' an' when yer dreamin'? "

And Mike looked up with a smile that was half cheerful, half pathetic.

" Well, scarcely to that extent, Mike," was the answer.

" Ah! no; likely not," Mike replied: " only folks as never had but one glad 'appy thing in the world, an' lost that, feels in that way, I specks."

" Very likely, Mike; but no good can come of always brooding over what is lost."

" Oh, don't you go a-thinking," he said, looking up suddenly, " that I'm always a-frettin' an' repinin' over what is past an' gone. Nowt of the sort. 'Tain't gone either, in one way. I've only to shut my eyes an' it's with me again. Didn't I tell yer it was a piece of myself ? That old home back there in th' country 'll never go away while I lives. It may be pulled down till there ain't two stones left of it, but nobody can never pull it out of my heart, don't 'e see ? " And Mike smiled as brightly as if all the wealth of the world were his.

" Mike, you are a philosopher," was the reply.

" I don't know what ph'losopher are," he said laughing ; " but I knows very well that I ain't lost anythink I had out-an'-out. I've got the—the—think of it—aye, mem'ry of it, that's the word. I've got the mem'ry of it left ; aye, an' more'n that, by a long chalk. Why, only last night it were all as real as ever. Mos' likely I was dreamin' ; daresay 1 were "——

Here Mike paused as if his thoughts had suddenly gone miles away from his present surroundings.

" Well, Mike," we ventured to remark, " what was your dream about ? "

" Oh, aye ! " he said with a little start, a sudden smile lighting up his face like a gleam of sunshine. " I s'pose it were a dream—no doubt ; but 't were all as real as life. I was lyin' in my little bed—I never told yer 'bout that bed, did I ? It were pawned to pay the rent, but I were in it again las' night—an' wide awake—aye, as wide awake as I be now : at least, it seemed so. I heard mother a-singin' downstairs, when the wind was quiet, as 'appy as a bird. I could hear the very words she were a-singing,—

> " ' Give to the winds thy fears,
>   Hope and be undismayed ;
> God hears thy sighs and counts thy tears
>   God shall lift up thy head.'

Then the wind began to come up from th' wood louder an' louder, but mother's voice kept above it for a bit, clear as a thrush,—

> " ' Through waves, and clouds, and storms,
>   He gently clears my way.'

Then the wind burst out a reg'lar roar, an' I heard the trees a-tossin' about their arms like anythink, an' mother's voice were lost altogether; then it got quieter an' quieter, till I could hear the old clock a-tickin' on th' stairs as plain as anythink—tick, tock, tick, tock, it went on. Then mother beginn'd again. I know'd the words in a minute, I'd heard her sing 'em so often,—

> " ' Fixed on this ground will I remain,
>   Though my heart fail and flesh decay;
> This anchor shall my soul sustain
>   When earth's foundations melt away ;
> Mercy's full power I then shall prove,
>   Loved with an everlasting love.'

" Nice words, ain't 'em ? "

" Yes, Mike, very nice."

" Ah, mother were 'mazin' fond of singin', an' she know'd such heaps of verses ; but she didn't sing so much after we got to Manchester, an' when she did sing it was sad like, not 'appy an' joyful like she used to sing. Dear old mother ! I've only to shut my

P

eyes, an' I'm wi' her again. Back among th' hills an' green fields, with the wind a-singin' in the trees."

"You don't dream much about Manchester, then, Mike?"

"Not if I knows it," he said brightly. "Yer see, it were all trouble in Manchester, from beginnin' to end. In the first place, father got a bit unsteady, as I may say. I don't think he hardly know'd it hisself, an' mother never blamed him very much. When his day's work in the stuffy cellar were done, he'd no green fields to go into, an' there seemed no comfort for him anywheres but at the public. He used to tell mother about a place where there was a great big room, an' plenty of gaslights, an' easy-chairs, an' all sorts of newspapers, an' a great fire in the winter, an' plenty of company; an' mother didn't seem to have the heart to complain of his goin', an' so he took to goin' reg'lar, every night a'most. An' things got worse wi' us all the while.

"He seemed to give up all hope of bein' any better off in the world, or of havin' any nicer home, an' then he were never very strong, an' half his time didn't seem to have no heart for work or anythink else. So things were allowed to drift as they liked.

"Mother an' me had to keep the house goin' as best we could. I couldn't get very much as a reg'lar thing. Sometimes I'd have a run of luck, but it 'ud never last very long, an' poor mother worked herself a'most to a shadow. She never got to bed sca'ce till midnight, a-stitchin' all the time, an' most nights I used to sit up wi' her readin' aloud. I were always quick at readin', an' old Gracey Diggle let me have plenty of stuff to read.

"I never told you 'bout Gracie, did I? Well, she were a brick, were Gracey. She lived right down th' end of our street, 'gin Oldham Road, an' kept a little newspaper-shop. I used to take out newspapers for her every mornin', and once a month I took out her magazines, *Chambers' Journal,* an' *Sunday at Home,* an' sichlike. She didn't give me much money for doin' it, but she let me read as many papers as I liked, so long as I kept 'em clean; an' she got a lot of sewin' for mother into th' bargain; so she were a real friend, were Gracey.

"I was 'mazin' fond of readin' *The Young English Gent,* an' *The Boys of the Empire,* an' sichlike papers. I should never ha' thought of the sea but for readin' them papers. An' they made it out so fine too, an' told sich grand stories, as if sea-life were the grandest fun in the world. I don't think them as wrote the stories know'd owt about it. An' if they did, they were very wicked to tell sich lies.

"Well, I used to read to mother durin' the long evenin's, an' it helped to pass the time away, an' made us forget the dingy room we were in. But it puffed me up wi' fancies I'd better never ha' had.

"One Saturday night, I mind it very well, I'd been readin' a story 'bout the sea which I thought was mighty fine, when the clock in the steeple began to strike, an' mother counted the strokes.

"'Twelve o'clock,' said she, startin' up, an' father not home; I wonder where he is.' For he were always home by eleven o'clock, or a minute or two after.

"Mother would do no more work after that, for she never did any sewin' on a Sunday. So we kept a-waitin' and a-listenin' for father's footsteps; but he didn't come, an' mother got to look quite scared an' anxious. At last we heard a strange footstep outside, an' a moment after a loud rat-tat-tat on the door.

"Mother started up in a moment, tremblin' all over, for she fear'd directly that there was somethink wrong. When she opened the door there was a big p'leeceman a'most fillin' the doorway.

"'Is this where John Barlow lives?' says he.

"'Yes, sir,' says mother, a-tremblin' more than ever, an' as white as a sheet.

"'Are you Mrs. Barlow, then?' he asked.

"'Yes,' said mother, though she could hardly get out the word, she were that skear'd.

"'Then I've come to tell you,' said the p'leeceman, that yer husband's been apprehended for takin' part in a row, an' a case of woundin', in Ancoats.

"'Apprehended?' says I. 'Is that took up?'

"'Yes,' says the p'leeceman larfin'; 'he's been took up, if yer like it better.'

"'An' is my husband in prison?' said mother, looking a'most ready to drop.

"'Yer husband's at the p'leece-station,' said he, 'where he will remain till Monday, when he'll be brought before the magistrates.'

"'Oh, dear!' says mother, 'I'm sure there must be some mistake. John would never hurt anybody.'

"'I can assure you, marm,' said the p'leeceman, proud like, 'that there's no mistake at all; so I wish yer a very good night.'

" Well, mother seemed knocked all of a heap, an' stood starin' out into the dark street as though her wits had cleared off altogether.

" ' What shall us do, mother ? ' says I at last.

" An' then she quietly shut the door, an' comed back an' sat down; but she did not speak, an' the look upon her face I'll never forget to my dyin' day.

" We did not go to bed that night, neither on us we stay'd there till mornin', an' mother scarcely spoke for the night; but when the light of the day comed in I looked at her face, an' it seem'd to me she had grown years older sin' the night before.

" Soon as it were broad day she put on her bonnet an' shawl, an' went out.   She didn't tell me where she were a-goin'.   I axed her when she were puttin' on her shawl, but she did not speak.

" ' May I go with you, mother ? ' says I.

" ' No, Mike,' she says, an' then she kissed me.

" ' I'd rather go with you, mother,' I says.

" ' I'd rather not,' she says ; ' stay here an' keep the kettle boilin' till I come back—there's a good boy.'

" I thought she were going to come back no more, an' I got terribly frighten'd as hour after hour passed away an' she did not come; but I kept the kettle boilin' all the same.

" It was gettin' well on in the afternoon when she comed in, quiet like an' sudden.   ' Oh, Mike ! ' she gasped, and then fell right down on the floor.   I thought she were dead, she looked so white ; an' I darted off in a moment for Gracey Diggle.

" She soon got round after Gracey comed.   She'd only fainted, for she hadn't eaten nothink for the day.

She'd been tryin' to find out where father was, an' get to see him. She hadn't seen him, though.

"Next mornin' she was off again; an' I locked the door an' left the key with Gracey, an' went out to try to git a copper or two. I was lucky too, an' got thirteen pence by evenin'. Mother was sittin' by the fire when I got back, busy wi' her sewin'.

"She'd seen father, she said, but not to speak to, an' that he'd been remanded for three days.

"I didn't know what that were, but I thought it were likely somethin' good, as she seemed a bit more cheerful.

"She was allowed to see father afterwards. I wasn't with her, but father told her he were quite innocent—that he'd never lifted a finger in the row He were only in the room where the row took place, an' tried his best to git out of it. But some of 'em swore false, an' the man who were hurt swear'd that he see father wi' a knife in his hand.

"He must ha' been mistook in that, for father never carried a knife wi' him. Mother was quite sartin sure that father were innocent. But that didn't make no difference, leastways not to him; but it made a lot of difference to her. She couldn't a' bear'd it if she'd believ'd he were guilty.

"'Oh, Jack,' she said, 'all this comes of keepin' bad company. If you'd only come home in the evenin's, like you used to do before we com'd to this horrid city, we should ha' been saved all this trouble.'

"That were about the only time she blamed him; 'an then it came too late, I reckon, to do any good to him or her.'

CHAPTER IV.

LITTLE MAY.

"AND was your father acquitted?" I ventured to ask at length, for Mike had relapsed into silence; and his eyes had caught that dreamy wistful expression which had become so common of late, and which signified that he was wandering in dreamland again with the sunlight of childhood's years shining all around him.

"Acquitted?" he said, looking up with a little start; "you mean let off. Oh, no, he was not let off. They give'd him twelve months. Yer see, though he didn't take part in the row, he was in it all the same. But 't weren't right that he should ha' been punished for the wrong-doin' of others: do yer think so?"

" No, Mike, it does not seem right ; and yet it often happens in this world. If people do wickedly they not only suffer themselves, but they bring suffering upon those around them, and often upon those least able to bear it."

" Aye, that are so," he replied quickly. " Father did wrong in spending his time and money in the public ; an' mother an' me an' little May had to suffer for it."

" And your father, by associating with those people at the public-house, suffered for *their* wrong-doing."

" Aye, aye," he chimed in ; " as I always said to mother, the best side of a public-house were the outside."

" Quite true, Mike. But how did you get on after your father was sent to prison ? "

" Oh, purty middlin' for a month or two," he replied " Yer see, father had brought home sca'ce nothin' for a long time ; he found hisself in wittles, that's about all. So we weren't very much wuss off, you see. Besides, I got a sitiwation the week after as hoffice-boy, wi' a salary of three bob a week, an' chance of increase if trade mended. If I could only ha' stuck to it I'd ha' made my fortin' ; but—well, it com'd about in this way :

" Father'd been in prison 'bout three months when little May was born. Weren't she a little beauty though ! I've never seen such a little picter in all my born days ! an' as good as she were purty. Bless yer ! she sca'ce never cried, but 'ud lie on her back all day long, a-kicking up her 'eels, an larfin' an' crowin as 'appy as a bird !

" But poor mother took a bad turn, an were never herself no more. For three months after little May was born she never done a stitch of work, an' but for Gracey Diggle I reckon she must ha' died. It took all as I could earn to find food, an' then there was nothin' to pay the rent; an' when everythink in the house we could spare had been pawned, the landlord turned us out.

" We'd never ha' gone into Charter Street if we had know'd what sort of a place it were ; but I found a cheap cellar-room to let there, an' we was glad to put our heads in anywheres. It were a sad come-down from our little home in the country ; but we know'd it were no use a-complainin', though mother couldn't help frettin' sometimes.

" May were about six months old when we went into Charter Street, an' the purtiest little thing in Manchester. Gracey said she were like a wax doll, she were that fair and delicate-lookin'.

" I were always as pleased as anythink, when business were over, to get home to May. An' didn't she brighten up when I got home ! Bless yer, she know'd me as well as anythink, an' 'ud larf an' kick an' crow the minute I came in at the door.

" She never took to father, though. Strange, weren't it ? An' yet I don't know, neither. Yer see, she'd never seen him till she were nine months old, an then he never made nothin' of her.

" I mind the day father came home very well. Mother went to meet him to show him the way, for of course he didn't know we'd moved into Charter Street. I don't know how mother managed to walk so far, an' carry little May; for she were very weak, an' looked little more than a shadow.

"I didn't know father when I got home, he were that altered. He had long whiskers an' curly hair afore he were sent to gaol, but it were all cut off when he comed out. He didn't look like hisself at all.

"I told mother that I thought there'd been a mistake, an' that they'd sent us the wrong father. But she only smiled, sad like. She never smiled 'appy now, like she used to do.

"It always seems to me as if father died that day when the p'leeceman comed to tell us that he were took up. I reckon I can't make my meaning very plain: but I can't get it out of my head, that that mornin' when he went away were the last time I ever seen him—the father that comed back to us from the prison never seem'd him.

"'Yer father's very much alter'd, Mike,' mother said to me one mornin' a few days after he come back. 'He's been suffering unjustly for twelve months, and it's sour'd him very much.'

"'He don't seem like father at all,' I said.

"She smiled a bit, an' said, 'I should know him among a million, Mike. But I don't deny he's greatly changed; he owns to it himself, an' I feel quite afraid of him sometimes. He said last night that the wrongs he had received had made him a devil—that's the very word he used.'

"I didn't know what to say, so mother went on: 'He's been broodin' over his wrongs all the year, night an' day, an' it's made him mad. He says it don't matter what becomes of him: that he's a marked man, a gaol-bird; that the p'leeceman knows him an' have their eye on him; an' that there's never a chance more for him in life.'

" ' I'm 'fraid that's very true, mother,' I said.

" ' I don't know what'll become of us,' she said with a sigh; 'at least I don't know what'll become of you, an' little May, an' him. As for myself, I shall soon be out of it all.'

" ' Out of it all, mother!' I said; 'what d'ye mean?'

" ' I mean what I say, Mike,' she answered; an' she smoothed my hair with her hand, an' oh, how thin it were an' white! 'I'm not sorry for myself,' she went on, with a little shake in her voice, 'but the thought of leavin' you nearly breaks my heart.'

" ' But, mother, I said, 'you'll not leave us yet for many a year; an' when I gets bigger, I'll earn lots of money, an' we'll have a little house in the country again yet, an' then you'll be as happy as a bird.'

" ' My poor Mike,' she said, an' she drew me closer to her, an' put her arm round me, an' tapped my back softly with the ends of her fingers. She didn't speak for a long time, but I felt the tears fallin' on the top of my head; and I couldn't speak myself, my heart was that full.

" It's best you should know, Mike,' she said, after a long while, an' her voice were very quiet and sad, 'its best you should know an' be prepared. I shall soon be sleeping quietly, Mike, where troubles never come, an' where hearts never ache no more. I've battled agin' the feelin' as long as I'm able, but it's no use. If it weren't for you an' May I'd be glad to go, for I'm nothin' to your father now, and he'd do as well with-

out me. I hoped, when little May was born, that
she'd die an' go to heaven; but the good God knows
best. But you must take care of her, Mike, when I
am gone. Maybe she won't trouble you very long,
for she's a frail little flower; but don't lose sight of
her, Mike, and the good God will help you somehow.'

" 'Oh, mother,' I said sobbin', for I couldn't keep
from cryin' any longer, ' don't talk in that way.
Maybe God will let you stay. You've told me
hundreds of times that the Lord was good, an' so has
teacher at the ragged school, an' p'r'aps, if we ax Him
very hard He'll let you stay.'

" 'I have axed Him, Mike,' she said, quietly tapping
my back wi' her fingers, ' axed Him in agony and wi'
tears. But I know now that His will is that I should
go; an' however hard it may be, I know His will is
best.'

" 'How do yer know it's His will, mother ? ' I said.

" Because I have the feelin' in me, Mike,' she
answered, 'an' it grows and grows every day. I cannot make it any plainer to you, Mike. But I knows
I shall soon be gone. I may last till the spring-time
comes, and the flowers bloom again; but I shall never
see them, nor see the dear country any more. If I
could ha' died in the old home, with the singin' of the
breeze in my ears, an' the smell of the flowers comin'
up from the garden, and the twittering of the birds
outside, an' then be buried in the dear old churchyard
where Sam, an' Peter, an' Eunie sleep, I think I'd be
content. But it cannot be, an' I do not want to
murmur.'

" Then she broke down an' begin to cry; an' I cried

with her, for I know'd then that all she were a-tellin
me were true.

"'I didn't think,' she said after a bit, 'that I
should have ended my days in a cellar. Your father
an' I loved each other very dearly when we were wed,
and we were very happy up to the time old Mr.
Naylor died, though your father had begun to change
long before that; but I didn't think any of us 'ud
have come to this.'

"And she began to cry again.

"I lost heart for everything nearly after that. I
didn't even care for readin', though I had lots of time,
an' Gracey was as kind as ever in lendin' me papers.
But as soon as ever I begins to read, mother's white
face 'ud come somehow between my eyes an' the
paper, an' the words 'ud all run together of a heap.
An' when I got home in the evenin's, the sight of little
May would make me think of all mother told me, an'
her laugh 'ud go through my heart like a knife.

"I don't think father done any work sca'ce after he
comed out of prison. He got a place or two; but as
soon as the folks found out he'd been in gaol he had
to walk it in quick sticks. It were very hard on him.
Yer see, if he wanted to be good an' honest, folks
wouldn't give him the chance.

"I dunno how he spent his time, nor where he
picked up the money to get drink wi'. We saw
precious little of him at home: he'd go away on a
Monday mornin' sometimes, an' we shouldn't see anythink more of him till Friday or Saturday. What
poor mother thought of it I don't know, but she said
very little; but I fancy she were a-troublin' more

about May an' me than she were about him, for she know'd the end were comin' nearer every day, an' her heart were very sore at the thought of leavin' us.

" 'T were a very mild winter, an' that were a great mercy, for our clothes were very thin an' poor, an' we could only afford to have the leastest bit of fire. Mother didn't seem no worse, an' I had a bit of hope sometimes that she'd mend when spring comed on.

" I mind Christmas Day very well. I was pleased as anythink to have a holiday, so that I could be home wi' mother an' May. I was indoors all day 'cept a bit in the afternoon, when I went down to the ragged school, where we'd some singin', and an' orange each. I got a extra orange for May, an' right pleased I was to git back home again.

" Well, we were sittin' together afore the fire in the evenin, enjoyin' our oranges, when "———

But here Mike paused, while a look of pain swept over his face, and in his eyes there was a troubled expression, as though the memories of the past were too painful to be recalled just then.

CHAPTER V.

DARKNESS.

MIKE was so visibly affected that I did not press him for a continuation of his story, and for several days had not the opportunity of seeing him again. He had quite regained his cheerfulness, however, on the occasion of our next meeting, and plunged into the recital of his story as though it were an agreeable diversion.

"I were a-tellin' you 'bout that Christmas Day, weren't I?" he went on. "I mind when we lived in the country we used to have a big bonfire on Christmas Eve, an' cocoa an' bun-loaf, an' we used to put bits of box an' holly behind the picters, an' round the clock, an' have a kind of jollification, like; an' then on Christmas Day we used to have plum-puddin' for dinner, an' a good slice of beef. But, oh lor', that were all altered when we got to Manchester. We never seen no holly, 'cept in the market, an' I seen 'em chargin' sixpence for jist a handful of it.

"Ah, well, we'd no holly or plum-puddin' in Charter Street, you may depend, an' precious little to eat; an' as for goin' to church to hear 'em sing

'Christians awake, salute the 'appy morn,'

why, that were jist onpossible, cause as how we'd no clothes fit to be seen in, an' yer see we'd never been used to goin' to church shabby-like.

"If 't weren't for the ragged school, I shouldn't ha gone nowhere on the Sunday. But, yer see, at the ragged school I weren't noticed, 'cause as how there were lots of other childer raggeder than me. An' our teachers were jist as kind to us as if we was fine gentry.

"Well, as I was a-tellin' yer, we was sittin' by the fire, mother an' May an' me, enjoyin' the horanges that I had brought home wi' me, when there comed all of a sudden a hard rat-tat on the door.

"Mother jumped up in a moment as white as a sheet, then dropped down into her chair again.

"'You go an' open the door, Mike,' she said, all gaspy like; 'I wonder who it can be!'

"I didn't say nothin', but went at once an' opened

the door, expectin' to see a big p'leeceman afore me, for I thought very likely father'd got took up again.

" 'T weren't a p'leeceman though, but a railway porter, as we found out after. He didn't speak for a moment; he were thinkin' how to begin, I reckon. Then he said, quiet like,—

" ' Does Mrs. Barlow live here, my lad ? '

" ' Yes,' I says ; ' do yer want her ? '

" ' Well, yes,' he said, speakin' very slowly. ' I've somethin' to tell her.'

" ' Ax the gentleman to come in,' called out mother ; but she didn't git up from her chair.

" So he comed in an' stood agin' the fire, an' rested his shoulder agin' the mantelpiece, an' twisted his cap about in his hands ; but he didn't speak. I guessed mother know'd there were somethin' up, for her eyes looked quite wild like, and her lips moved several times as if she wanted to say somethin' ; but she kep' silent all the same.

" Well, thinks I, this is a queer go. I wonder what the man wants a-twiddlin' his cap about that way without speakin'. So I jist up an' axes him right out what he'd got to say to mother.

" ' Oh ! ' he says, lookin' straight into the fire, ' I'm the bearer of a message, Mrs. Barlow, an', I'm sorry to say, an unpleasant one.'

" ' Tell me the worst at once,' says mother, comin' out with the words all of a sudden.

" ' It's about yer husband, ma'am,' says the man.

" ' Yes, I know,' says mother, as though she were in a passion like. ' What is it—what's he been doin' ? '

" ' I can assure you, ma'am,' said he, ' that no blame

Q

rests wi' the company in the matter ; he would persist
in gettin' out before the train stopped.'

" ' What do you mean ? ' said mother, startin' up
from her chair. ' Is he hurt—killed—what is it ?
Do tell me.'

" ' Yes, ma'am, he's hurt—badly hurt, I should say,
ma'am. But don't give way more than you can help,'
said the man, quite feelin' like.

" ' You ain't told me all,' said mother, quite fierce
like. ' My husband's dead, you know he is.'

" ' Oh, no, ma'am. It's not so bad as that, I hope,'
said he ; ' he could speak when he were got out, an'
told who he was and where he lived.'

" ' Then where is he ? ' said mother, and she stood
straight up tall before the man. ' Where is he, an'
why isn't he brought here ? '

" ' They've taken him to the infirmary, ma'am, and '—

" But mother didn't stop to hear any more. She
seemed to git strong all of a sudden, an' almost before
I knowed what she were doin', she'd got on her bonnet
an' shawl an' were out of the house. She called back
from the door, ' Look after May, Mike,' an' then she
was off like a shot.

" Dear little May didn't know nothin' about it, an'
were as 'appy as a cat in the sunshine, an' as good as
gold. I got her on my lap when mother was gone,
an' 'lowed her to pull my hair an' push her purty little
fingers into my eyes. She were asleep, though, afore
mother got home ; so I put her to bed an' tucked her
in warm for the night.

" I don't know how long mother were away ; p'r'aps
two hours, p'r'aps more. But I never seed a face like

hers when she comed home. She didn't say nothin';
she just dropped down on her knees by the side of the
bed, an', pushin' her face agin' the clothes, begin to cry.
I'd seen her cry many times afore, but never like that.

" ' What is it, mother ? an' how's father ? ' I says
to her ; but I don't think she heard me. She only
sobbed more violent than ever.

" I got so frightened at last—she cried so hard, an'
wouldn't notice nothink—that I went an' fetched
Gracey.

" Then she got quieter after a bit, an' the first words
she spoke were, ' Oh, Gracey, he's gone.'

" ' Who's gone ? ' says Gracey, for I hadn't told her
nothink about it.

" ' My husband,' says mother.

" ' Gone where ? ' says Gracey, lookin' surprised like.

" ' Ha ! ' she said with a gasp, as if Gracey's words
had stabbed her.

" Then she opened her eyes very wide, an' stared
all round the room ; an' I'll never forget her look to
my dyin' day.

" ' What is it ? ' said Gracey ; ' an' where's he gone
to ? '

" ' He's gone—to—*God*,' says mother, speakin' the
last word in a whisper.

" ' Goodness gracious ! ' said Gracey, lookin' as white
as a ghost. ' You don't mean to say he's dead ? '

" ' Yes,' says mother, speakin' very quiet, ' he died a
few minutes after I got there, with his head upon my
shoulder.'

" ' Got there ! ' says Gracey. ' Got where ? What
does it all mean ? '

" Then mother told her all : how father was tipsy, an' would get out of the carriage when it were comin' swift into the station, an' how the wheels went over him.

" ' He were quite conscious,' mother said, ' an' smiled on me like he used to do in the old days. " Kiss me, my gal," he says, " for it's all over with me." An' I put my arm around his neck an' kissed him. " Raise me a bit," he says, after a moment or two ; an' those were the last words he spoke. He just smiled after I had raised his head, an' were gone.'

" Gracey stayed wi' us all night, an' I know she were a great comfort to mother, an' to me too ; for she were always cheerful, were Gracey, an' always kind.

" I don't know what mother was like after father was buried. Half her time she seemed as if she were in a dream. She didn't fret very much, but she never smiled—or scarcely never.

" Sometimes when I spoke to her she'd start as though somebody fired off a gun by her ear ; an' when she looked at me or Gracey, I don't b'lieve she'd see us half her time. There was sich a curious look in her eyes, as if she were a-looking through you an' seein' somebody miles away behind you.

" I faniced sometimes when I got home in the evenin' that she'd been cryin' ; but she didn't cry afore me, an' she never talked about father if she could help it.

" One day I axed her what she meaned when she told Gracey that father was gone to God. But I didn't understand it very well when she explained. Do you understand it ? "

" I don't know what explanation she gave, Mike."

" Oh, she said as how God made all our spirits, and that when we died our spirits went back to Him."

" And what reply did you make ? "

" Oh, I didn't say nothin' at all, for I couldn't see through it quite. I know'd that father weren't a prayin' man, an' I don't think he was prepared to die. But I thought likely if he'd gone to God, that God 'ud do right wi' him. You think God will, don't you ? ' and Mike looked up with a questioning expression in his eyes.

" There is no doubt of that, Mike. God is good, and just, and will do no wrong to any one, and we may contentedly leave the spirits of all men with Him."

" Aye, I guess that's so," said Mike. " Mother always said as how God were our Father, an' that He'd do everythink for the best, an' make no mistakes.

" It were a great comfort for her to think that way too," he went on. " She know'd all the while that she was goin' away to God herself, an' were leavin' little May and me behind to fight the world as best we could ; an' 't were very nice for her to think there 'ud be somebody to look after us, an' keep a eye upon us.

" I used to wake up in the night sometimes, and hear her prayin' to the good Lord for May an' me. I don't think she slept very much ; she didn't seem to want it. Maybe she thought of the long sleep as were a-comin', an' so were anxious to do as much work afore she went as were possible.

" She worked very hard too, an' didn't seem to eat as much as little May, an' I know'd she couldn't last very long that way. I tried sometimes to get her to eat a bit more, but 't were no go——she couldn't get it down.

"An' so she got whiter an' thinner an' weaker all the while. But she kep' battlin' on. Little May were her great comfort an' her great sorrow, if you can make that out. Nobody can tell how dear the little gal was to her heart, nor how big was the grief, that she'd have to die an' leave her behind. I used to see her sometimes lookin' at the little gal wi' eyes that looked fair hungry, an' I know'd she were a-wonderin' what 'ud become of the little angel when she were a-sleepin' under the turf.

"When I think of it now, I wonder how she kep' up as long as she did. Gracey said 't was her spirit that kep' her a-going. But 't were a sad time for all of us. It nearly broke my heart to see her droopin' like a flower in the autumn. Sometimes I thought if I could only get her out into the country, she'd rally and get well again; for the air were foul in Charter Street, an' never a breeze durin' the summer got into our cellar, an' in the winter 't was damp an' cold.

"But what were the use thinkin' about the country? There were no more country for her in this world. I know'd that very well; an' the thought of the green fields, an' the daisies a-bloomin', an' the buttercups a-shinin' in the sun, only made me mad.

"'T were a beautiful spring too. Leastaways it must ha' been in the country. We never got none of it in Charter Street, not even the sight of a primrose or a blade of grass. We got the sunshine, 'tis true: that goes everywhere.

"If I ever spoke to mother about the country, she'd

smile ever so sweetly, an' say she'd soon be in the country now, where the flowers 'ud be always in bloom, an' the chill of the winter 'ud never come. So I didn't often say anythink to her about it, for I couldn't bear to hear her talkin' that way.

" Well, well; I guess I'm takin' a long time to tell my story, but I didn't think there were so much to tell till I begun. But I must hurry on, for I've a good bit more yet to tell."

CHAPTER VI.

THE DARKNESS DEEPENS.

"SHE went in the spring, as she said she would. Leastways, it was in May, an' that's spring, I reckon. Up to 'bout a fortnight afore she went she didn't seem to get no worse, an' I couldn't help hopin' a bit sometimes she'd rally maybe when the summer came. But *she* know'd better.

"'Mike,' she says to me, 'I've gived you an' little May to God. Night an' day I ain't ceased to pray to Him, that He'd take care of you when I'm no more. An' I think He's answered me, for I don't worry about you now. You may think it's very strange, but all trouble's gone out of my heart.'

"'I'm glad you don't trouble, mother,' I says, 'for I

b'lieve God an' me 'll be able to take care of little May atween us.'

" ' My poor Mike,' she says, ' you'll need a-takin' care of almost as much as little May. But I hope, when you get bigger, you'll be able to get away out of this great city, an' live with your little sister somewhere in the quiet country. I've always dreaded the thought of May growing up in this sinful place. But that's gone now, an' God 'll take care of you.'

" I didn't say nothink to that, for I was near a-chokin', an' I didn't want her to see as how my heart was breakin' all the while.

" So she kept on a-talkin', quiet like an' sad.

" ' You'll live with Gracey,' says she, ' when I'm sleepin' in the dust. Gracey's been very good, an' she's promised to do her best by you. Maybe I'll be able to look down on you from the sky an' see how you are gettin' on. But you'll never lose sight of May, Mike ? '

" ' Never, mother,' says I, turnin' away my head.

" ' You've always been a good boy, Mike,' she says, strokin' my hair with her thin white hand. ' You've never been no trouble to me, or anxiety, an' you mustn't fret for me when I'm gone. I shall be better off, Mike, in the land where there's no more pain.'

" ' I couldn't keep it back no longer after that. So I just throw'd my arms 'bout her neck an' burst out sobbin'.

" ' Oh, mother ! ' I says, ' I cannot let you go ; I'll break my heart an' die, I know, if you are taken ; an how can God be good to take you away, when we've nobody in the world but you ? '

" ' Hush, Mike, my darling,' she says, quickly, ' you don't know what you are a-sayin'. But you'll see things better by an' by.'

" Dear old mother! We didn't have many more talks after that. She went away quiet one evening, soon after the sun set.

" I'd got home a little earlier than usual, and little May met me at the door. Purty little creature; she could run about as nimble as anythink, and talk— Gracey said — like a parrot; only Gracey couldn't always make out what she said.

" ' Is that you, Mike ?' said mother, as soon as I got inside the door.

" ' Aye, mother,' says I, goin' up to the bedside ; for she were lyin' down, so I guessed she didn't feel so well.

" ' I'm feelin' very tired an' strange,' she said. ' I think I'll try an' sleep a bit. But I'd like to hear you sing again that new hymn you learn'd at the ragged school, Mike. Sing it soft, my child, an' I think I'll drop off,' an' she smiled upon me ever so sweetly.

" So I beginned to sing, for she didn't look no worse, an' I was glad to please her :

> ' In heavenly love abiding,
>   No change my heart shall fear,
> And safe in such confiding,
>   For nothing changes here.
> The storm may roar without me,
>   My heart may low be laid,
> But God is round about me,
>   And can I be dismayed ?'

" ' That is very beautiful,' she said, ever so quietly ' sing on, my Mike. to the end.'

" So I kept singin' on :

> ' Wherever He may guide me,
>   No want shall turn me back ;
> My Shepherd is beside me,
>   And nothing can I lack.
> His wisdom ever waketh,
>   His sight is never dim,
> He knows the way He taketh,
>   And I will walk with Him.

> ' Green pastures are before me,
>   Which yet I have not seen ;
> Bright skies will soon be o'er me,
>   Where the dark clouds have been.
> My hope I cannot measure,
>   My path to life is free,
> My Saviour has my treasure,
>   And He will walk with me.'

" She must ha' dropt off while I were singin', as she expected. So, not wishin' to disturb her, I took little May in my arms an' went out, an' sat in the doorway. Poor little May ! she were as light as a feather a'most, but as merry as a cricket for all that.

" 'T weren't dark by a good bit. But the dark were a-beginnin' to come on. We must a-stayed there a goodish bit; for 't were nearly dark when we looked up, and there was Gracey afore us.

" ' What are 'e doin' here, sittin' in the dark ? ' she says.

" ' Mother's sleepin',' says I, ' an' we didn't want to disturb her.'

" ' But it's time you were in the house,' says she, an' she went in an' lighted a candle. I thought she gived a bit of a cry, but I couldn't be sartin ; but the candle went out in a moment, an' she comes to me an' says,—

"'Yer mother ain't had such a sleep as this afore an' I think I'll stay here a bit if you an' May 'll go an' mind the shop. Here's the key; you know the price of the papers, don't you? An' if May gets sleepy, put her in my bed.'

"She spoke quick like and anxious, but I didn't take much notice. So I takes the key an' catches up little May in my arms, an' off I goes.

"I don't know what time Gracey got home, for May was sleepin' in Gracey's bed, an' I were sound asleep in her rockin'-chair; an' she let me sleep on till mornin'. She didn't say anythink 'bout mother till after breakfast; then she told me."

There was a pause here, for Mike's voice had grown tremulous, while two tear-drops trembled on his eyelids, then rolled silently down his cheeks. He did not speak again for several seconds, nor did he seem conscious of his surroundings or of the flight of time; for into his eyes had stolen that dreamy far-away expression that we have already spoken of, which clearly indicated that his thoughts were wandering again in the chequered paths of other years.

"I never seen mother no more after that," he went on, as though there had been no pause. "Gracey were very good, an' 'tended to everythink."

"I reckon it must ha' been 'bout two days after. I'd come home to Gracey's house very tired, for I hadn't had no sleep since mother went. I found little May sittin' on the floor, cryin' for mother.

"'Oh, mother, do come to me!' she were a-sayin'; and

poor Gracey seemed at her wits' end. An' sorry enough, I reckon, that she'd undertook to look after May an' me.

"'Oh, here's Mike!' says little May, as soon as I comed in; an' she jumped up in a minute, an' comed runnin' to me as glad as a bird.

"Oh, you should ha' seen May! She were as purty as a dream an' as sweet as a flower.

"Well, I catches her up in my arms in a jiffy. 'Mike's darling,' says I, an' I dropped into Gracey's rockin'-chair wi' the little angel on my knee, an'— whether you b'lieve it or no, it's as true as I'm here—in less than five minutes we were both on us fast asleep.

"I don't no more know than Adam how long I were sleepin;' but I were waked up by voices talkin' in Gracey's little shop, an', squintin' through the little window, I seed two gentlemen talkin' wi' Gracey. One of 'em I knowed very well—he were Mr. Legg the parish man, an' had come to see mother a time or two afore she went; the other one I'd never seen before.

"'My good woman,' Mr. Legg were sayin', 'it's of no use in the world. The child is very weakly, and needs great care and attention; and I'm sure, with your kind heart, it will be a great relief to you to know the child is much better looked after than you could possibly look after her with your duties. As for the boy, he can sleep here if you greatly wish, but it would be better, I think, if you would allow my friend here, Mr. Smith, to find him a bed at the Refuge, which he is quite willing to do.'

"'Quite willing, my good woman,' said Mr. Smith; 'and I can assure you it would be much better that the lad should have proper training.'

"'But I promised their mother,' said Gracey.

"'Yes, we know,' they both said; 'and it's very good of you. But really the thing cannot be allowed.'

"'It 'ud be a great load off my mind,' said Gracey.

"'Of course; and this is the only way in which you can properly keep your promise and do your duty by them.'

"Then Gracey comed an' peeped in at the door, but I keeps my eyes shut; but they spoke quieter after that, an' I could only catch a word here an' there, but I made out that Gracey was to take little May somewheres the next day. I guessed it were to the workhouse, but p'r'aps I were wrong in that. I think sometimes maybe I was; I don't know. But one thing was sartin, little May was to be taken away from me.

"Do you think I could stand that, after what I'd promised mother? Could you a-stood it? I guess you don't know what it is to be put in a corner like that.

"I looked down on the little angel a-sleepin' so innercent in my arms, with the purtiest bit of a smile a-playin' 'bout her mouth, an' I said in my heart I'd die first—that we'd both die together.' Maybe I was wrong in that. I don't know. But I couldn't forget how mother asked me to promise that I'd never lose sight of May.

"After a bit the gentlemen went away, an' Gracey comed into the room an' beginned to stir the fire. But I didn't open my eyes for a goodish bit; an' May kept sleepin' on in my arms, breathin' as soft an' reg'lar as a kitten.

"At last May beginned to stir, and so I opened my eyes an' looked around me. 'I guess I've been noddin' a bit,' says I to Gracey.

" ' Why, you've had quite a long sleep,' said Gracey, ' an' I've been very glad to see it, for I'm sure you needed it very badly.'

" ' Aye,' I says, ' I ain't had a wink afore since poor mother went.'

" ' Poor boy,' says Gracey ; ' but it's time I were seein' about gettin' a bit of supper.'

" Then little May beginned askin' for mother again, an' wantin' to know why she kept away so long, an' I had terrible hard work to satisfy her too. When I told her mother was gone to a beautiful country, far away above the stars, she beginned to cry, an' said as how she wanted to go, an' nothin' would keep her quiet till Gracey had brought the supper in.

" I don't know how I managed to get down any supper, for my heart was up in my mouth a-choking me all the time ; but I forced it down, for I didn't want Gracey to think as how I'd heard anythink. Poor Gracey ! she mean'd all for the best, I know ; an' she were very kind. But I'd made my mind up ; an if I've giv'd her trouble, I'm very sorry.

" Gracey had made up a little bed for us downstairs she slept upstairs, so I know'd I could manage without very much trouble.

" While Gracey was in the shop I was busy gettin' things ready. An' when everythink was straight, I kneel'd down an' said my prayers, an' axed the good Lord to take care of me an' little May.

" When Gracey com'd to tuck us in I was lyin' with my eyes shut. An' little May was fast asleep by my side."

CHAPTER VII.

ON THE TRAMP.

I DIDN'T sleep that night, though; not a single wink.

"I lay a-watchin' and a-listenin', with my heart thumpin' agin my side as if it 'ud come through; an' when at length the first glimmer of day slipped in through the winder, I got up an' dressed myself. Little May were very sleepy at first; but when I told her we were goin' into the country, to see the birds an' flowers, an' all that, she were wide awake in no time, though I don't think she know'd very well what I were a-talkin' about.

"I were dreadfully afraid I should wake Gracey; but I don't think I did, and when once we'd got into the street I were off like a shot. Poor Gracey, I guess she were some skeared when she got up in the mornin' an' found we had cleared off. But I've never seen her since, so I don't know what she thought. I'd be mighty glad to see Gracey again. An' when I'm able to toddle so far, I mean to look her up.

"Well, as I were sayin', we were off pretty sharp, as you may guess. May was no weight sca'ce, an' all the clothes we had made a very small bundle. There was nobody about either. I don't think I seen two people between Gracey's house an' Miles Platting.

" I'd no notion in the world where I was goin' to.

" There was just one thought that fixed me, an' that was, to git away from Manchester. I thought, maybe when I got away so far, that the parish man 'ud have no chance of findin' me. I'd be able to find some way of lookin' after little May, an' finding bread for us both.

" I were awful sold that day, though. I thought I were goin' to git right away into the country, where there'd be big woods an' only a house here an' there; but bless you, sca'ce had the houses got to be a bit thin afore they got to be thicker again, an' before I'd fair left Manchester I'd got to Oldham!

" I guess you've no notion how tired I was of seein' streets, streets everywhere, nothin' but streets wherever I went. But I had to make the best of it. Well, I kept wanderin' round all the day, sittin' down on a doorstep to rest now an' then; for I got precious tired afore evenin', an' I was in sore trouble too, for I didn't know where we was to git a place to sleep.

" Well, it were gettin' on towards evenin' when I got a awful fright. Little May were fast asleep in my arms, and I were draggin' myself along precious slow, for I were nearly dead beat, when I feels a hand laid on my shoulder, an', lookin' up, there was a big bobby standin' right afore me.

" Oh, dear! I thought I should ha' gone right through the ground. I never did feel so queer in all my born days.

R

" ' Well, youngster,' said he, ' what ye mean by loiterin' about here in this way ? '

" ' I reckon I've lost my way,' says I, puttin' on as bold a face as I could, though I could scarcely speak for fright.

" ' Where'd you want to go to ? ' says he.

" ' To—to—Rochdale,' says I, coming out wi' the first place I could think on. ' Is it much farther ? '

" ' You'll never git to Rochdale to-night,' says he.

" ' Not get there ? ' says I ; an' I reckon he thought I were terribly cut-up 'bout it. ' Goodness, what's us to do, then ? '

" ' Well,' says he, rubbin' his chin, an' lookin' 'portant like, ' we might find room for 'e in the casual's ward.'

" ' Where's that ? ' says I.

" ' Oh, a little farther on,' says he.

" ' What sort of place is it ? ' says I

" ' Very nice,' says he ; ' clean as a new pin, an' good feedin' to boot.'

" Well, 't wern't so bad on the whole ; an' I can tell yer I hadn't laid down my head five minutes afore I was sleepin' as sound as a top ; for I were desperate tired, as you may be sure.

" Next mornin' we had a pretty middlin' breakfast, an' were told the nearest way to Rochdale. So off we starts again. Little May were very quiet ; she only wanted to know if we were goin' to see mother.

" I reckon thoughts of mother were in her dear little head all the while.

" We hadn't no trouble in gettin' plenty to eat an' drink. The sight of May's white face, so sweet an' purty, 'ud fetch a piece of bread an' butter almost anywhere.

" In the evenin' I axed a p'leeceman if it were far to Halifax, an' if he thought I'd be able to git there in time for bed ?

" Well, you should ha' seen how he stared, an' then he larfed so hard that he had to hold his sides. He comed round, however, after a bit, an' spoke sensible ; an' took us to a very good shop, where we stayed for the night, an' got well looked after, I can tell yer.

" Those bobbies ain't half bad fellows when you get to know 'em. I used to be awful frightened at 'em, an' kept out of their way as far as I could. But I got to know better in time, an' found some on 'em real friends. Bless you, these bobbies have hearts an' feelin's as well as other people. An' I know I'd got on badly without 'em.

" I'll not soon forget the day I left Rochdale. Afore evenin' I'd got right out among the hills ; an' weren't they grand, an' didn't the sight of them do me good ? I thought little May 'ud be pleased too, but she didn't seem to take much notice ; she only wanted to know if we were goin' to see mother. 'Twere always the same question with her. She wanted nothin' but mother.

" I were so pleased to be away from the smoke an' dirt of the town, that I didn't think how the day was goin' on. The weather were beautiful, too. An', oh, sich heaps of wild flowers ! an' in the afternoon we heard the cuckoo. Little May were pleased at that. An' butterflies ! I never seen such a sight. And when we got tired, we'd sit down on a soft bank, somewhere in the sunshine, an' listen to the birds singin', an' smell the flowers that were growin' all around us.

"May liked the streams the best. If I'd let her, she'd splash wi' her hands in them all the day; and if I hadn't watched her pretty close, she'd ha' splashed in 'em with her feet as well.

"But she didn't take no notice of the great hills all around; I suppose she weren't old enough to notice sich things.

"Well, as I was sayin', I didn't think how the day was goin' on, an', before I thought of it, it begun to get dark, an' there weren't a house in sight anywhere. I got pretty well skeared after a while, for I never mind it git dark so fast as it did that night. I didn't want for May to know that I was frightened, so I said nothin', but kept trampin' on; but it got darker an' darker all the while, an' the road got worse an' worse, till there was no road at all, an' I knowed then that I were lost."

"Was you ever lost, sir?"

"No, Mike."

"Oh, well; then I'm thinkin' you need never want to be."

"I were awful skeared I can tell yer; an' if little May hadn't been with me, I should ha' screamed an' shouted like anythink, I were that frightened. But little May, bless her, she were as good as gold, an' didn't seem to mind a bit; an' after a bit she nestled her head up agin me, and went fast asleep.

"Well, I tramped on as well as I could; an' that were bad enough, you may depend, for I were shakin' all over with fright. I don't know how long I kept goin' on—I thought 't were hours an' hours, but very likely 't weren't so much. But at last, all of a sudden my foot slipped, an' down I went into a pit. Leastways, I thought it were a pit then; but it turned out to be only a hollow in the hill-side.

' Well, I weren't hurt a bit, nor May either—you see I kept tight hold of her; an' if she waked up, she didn't say nothin', an' very soon after she were sleepin' again as sound as ever.

" Lucky for me I slipped on a soft place. There was plenty of moss, or bracken, or somethink of the sort all round, so I jist made up my mind to go no farther. I tucked in little May as warm as I could, an' made myself as comfortable as I was able, and waited.

" Well, it were queer, I can tell you. The country is grand and beautiful in the day-time, but it's mighty solemn in the night when you're all alone. I never want to be alone like it again. Overhead I could hear the wind whiskin' past, and whispering in the heather as solemn as a churchyard. Then everythink would become so still that I could hear my heart thumpin' away quite loud. Then the wind 'ud give a great sigh that 'ud fair startle me, an', but for wakin' little May, I should ha' screamed right out.

" Well, you may guess I were some pleased when I noticed that the darkness were gettin' thinner an' thinner; an' by an' by the light begun to shoot up in the sky, behind the hills—it *were* purty. I've never seen it so purty since. I wish I had words to tell it, but that ain't in my line.

"It got very chilly towards mornin'; my teeth fair chattered when I tried to speak, an' I'm afeared little May got cold. I don't know for sartin, but I fear so. Oh, dear! I didn't know what were comin', or I might ha' let 'em took little May to the work-house. I don't know. I wanted to do right, an' I tried; an' if I done wrong, I hope the good Lord 'll forgive me.

"It were the middle of the forenoon afore we got to a house, but the woman were very good to us, and gived us some warm bread an' milk; an' that night a p'leeceman found us a shop at a place they called Tormorden.

"But I needn't tell all the places we went to—I hardly know myself. But I kept hopin' all the while that somethink 'ud turn up, as little May an' me might have a home, an' I be able to get bread for both. But I were out of luck, somehow.

"I mind trampin' to Burnley, an' to Accrington, an' to Blackburn, an' Preston, an' Ormskirk, an' then I comed on here to Liverpool. In nearly all the places the bobbies were very good; an' that night I tell'd you of were the only one we spent out-of-doors.

"But little May got quieter every day, an' all her appetite went, till she didn't eat enough to keep a mouse alive. I were in sore trouble, an' tried every-think I could to amuse her; but 't were no go. She lay in my arms an' kept her eyes shut nearly all day long, takin' no notice of nothin'.

"I thought, when we got down on the landin'-stage, she would be pleased; but I couldn't get her as much as to open her eyes.

" By an' by the light began to shoot up in the sky."—Page 261.

" ' May,' says I, ' look at the shinin' water an' the beautiful vessels ; look, May, there's a darlin' ! ' but she didn't as much as move her eyelids.

" I couldn't make it out at all, for she'd always looked afore when I were very anxious she should. An' when I tried to move her, her head jist dropped on my arm, an' I couldn't rouse her nohow.

" I thought she must be very ill, so I kept her as close to me as I could, to keep her warm, for her little hands were cold as stones. I tried several times durin' the afternoon to rouse her ; but 't were all no use—she wouldn't smile on me, or speak, or anythink.

" Well, as it got on towards evenin' I went up to a p'leeceman,—for they were the only friends I had in the world,—an' I says to him,—

" ' I wish you could tell me what to do with little May, for I reckon she's awful ill.'

" ' Ill, eh ? ' says he ; ' let me look at her.'

" So I pulls back the shawl from her face, an' he looks at her for a moment. Then he touches her with the tip of his finger.

" ' Give her to me this minute,' says he, quite rough like. ' The child's dead.'

" ' 'T is a lie ! ' I screamed out ; for, oh, I couldn't believe that my little May had gone from me too.

" ' You'll have to answer for this,' said he, beckonin' to another p'leeceman to come. ' I wonder what you mean by carryin' a dead child around in your arms.'

" ' Oh, don't say she's dead ! ' I cried, for my

heart was quite broke.　　But he didn't take no notice.

"'Here, Bill,' says he, 'take this lad off to Dale Street.'　So I was walked off one way, while he took little May off another.

CHAPTER VIII.

A FRESH START.

"YOU was never in gaol, sir?"

"Oh, yes Mike, many times."

"Aye," with a bright smile overspreading all his face; "but not to stay there— not to be locked up?"

"Well, no: our experience of prisons is not quite so extensive as that."

"Oh, then you don't know nothink about it very much, I'm thinkin',"

" In that sense—no."

" But I oughtn't to grumble," he went on, " for they didn't take me to the proper gaol. I reckon they called it the p'leece-station, or somethink of the sort. But I were kept there the biggest part of a week altogether. An' I never seen little May no more; that were the hardest part of it all. I could ha' put up wi' all the rest, an' been happy, if only little May had been with me. But I never comed so near wishin' I were dead as I did then.

" You see, father, an' mother, and May had all gone in about six months, an' I were all alone in the world, without a friend or relation. I thought it were very hard ; an' sometimes I couldn't sca'ce pray a bit. I thought God couldn't care anythink about me, or He wouldn't ha' took away from me everythink I had to love.

" But I got more reconciled after a bit, when I had time to think it over quiet. I thought, maybe God was very good in takin' away the little angel from all the sufferin' and misery.

" You see, she were always wantin' to go to mother. Every mornin' she would say, ' S'all we see mother to-day, Mike ? ' I think those were the very last words I ever hear her spoke, an' sometimes they would cut into my heart like a knife.

" So, after a bit, I was able to say to myself, ' Mays' better off, an' I oughtn't to fret. She's wi' mother now, where she always wanted to be, an' mother 'll be glad, an' the Lord 'll look after 'em both, an' they'll be be very happy among the flowers of heaven.' But 't were very hard, for all that, to have to give her up, an' I cried myself to sleep every night for long enough after; though I know'd all the time that 't were for the best. For, you see, what could I ha' done with the little darlin'?' I hadn't no home nor anythink; an' I couldn't ha' tramped the world over, carryin' her in my arms.

"An' then I used to think, maybe I'd done wrong in not lettin' her go to the workhouse, or wherever the gentleman wanted her to be, for then she might ha' lived, an' I might ha' gone to see her sometimes; an' when I got to be a man she might keep my house, an' both on us live in the country. So I were sore boggled one way an' another; an' I used to pray very hard, that if I'd done wrong the dear Lord 'ud forgive me.

"Every day while I were in the p'leece-station I had to go before the bench or somewhere; an' sich heaps of questions were axed me, I thought they'd never ha' done. I was terribly frightened the first day, but after that I got more used to it; an' the gentlemen only wanted to find out the truth, an' that I was quite willin' to tell 'em.

"I don't think they know'd exactly what to do by me, an' so they kept me under their eye longer'n they might have done. However, in the end they told me I might go. So out I goes into the street, not knowin' which way to turn more'n the chap in the moon. It were very funny, too, not havin' little May to carry; an' though I felt freer, I were terribly down-hearted.

"Well, the first thing I had to do was to set to work an' try to earn a few coppers. An', you see, I weren't quite new at that kind of thing, an' I rubbed on very well for several weeks.

"But the sight of the great ships an' the river, an all that, brought back the longin' that had been in my heart for years, an' I made up my mind that, by hook or by crook, I'd go to sea. I thought of all the gran' stories that I'd read in Gracey's papers, an' I thought they must all be true; I b'leeved then that everythink that was in print were true, but I've learn'd different since. I wish now I had never seen *The Boys of the Empire*, an' sich like papers; then I shouldn't ha' heard the silly stories 'bout the fine times that boys have at sea. If I come across any boys as wants to be sailors, I'll tell 'em a story that'll put another face on it.

"Well, as I was a-saying, I was bent on bein' a sailor. An' I thought I'd like to go in one of the big steamers that I'd seen a-lyin' so grand in the river. They do look purty, too; an' very likely the sailors in 'em have better times than those in the small fry. I don't know, for I've never tried.

"But 't weren't a bit of use my trying to get on any of them first-raters. I found I'd have to begin at the beginnin' in bein' a sailor, as in everythink else. But 't weren't very easy for a poor lad who hadn't no friends to get a start at all.

"I kept knockin' 'bout the docks for weeks an' weeks, gettin' a odd job now an' then, an' livin' from hand to mouth. You see 't were summer-time, an' if I hadn't enough brass to pay for a night's lodgin', I could sleep out-of-doors.

"'T is a hard life, though; but I weren't alone. I

found scores of children, who hadn't no father nor mother any more'n me, an' who weren't as strong an' as well able to look after theirselves as I was. I guess there's a lot more trouble an' strugglin' in the world than most people think.

"I've wondered a lot lately whether the carriage-folk, when they drive through the grand streets, ever think that behind the tall houses there's courts an' alleys full of hungry little childer, an' all sorts of sufferin' an' misery an' awful want.

"But that ain't gettin' on with my story, is it? Well, I got took on at last. She were a smallish craft, four or five hundred tons or so, called *Nora*. She were takin' ballast to Swansea, where she was goin' to load a cargo of rail-iron for New Brunswick, then take back a load of timber to France somewhere, an' then anythink as might turn up. I didn't know all this when I were engaged; it comed out bit by bit.

"I mind the day very well when we left Liverpool. The weather were splendid, wi' just breeze enough to fill the sails and make everythink smell sweet. I was very proud, I can tell yer; an' yet my heart was very sad, an' I could hardly help cryin' sometimes when I thought of father an' mother an' May —all gone.

"I weren't altogether pleased either, for the sailors were nearly all drunk, an' the captain were cross as he could be, an' swore awful; but I thought likely 'nough they'd be all right by next day.

"On the whole, 't were a very good beginnin'. The weather kept fine an' the sea smooth, an' I weren't a bit sick all the way to Swansea. An' then we kept near the coast all the way; an' didn't Wales look beautiful, that's all! I seen old Snowdon wi' the sun rising behind, an' it did look very fine. I should like to see the country round from the top of that mountain —like Moses, you know, see the land of Canaan; but I guess I never shall now.

"It was near the end of September, I mind, afore we left Swansea, and we hadn't been out a week afore the trouble beginned. The fine weather broke up all of a sudden, an' we got westerly gales day after day. An', oh, sich seas! I was fair frightened when they broke over us from stem to stern, an' the vessel shivered and groaned as if she were going all to pieces.

"I was awful sick, too. Oh, I can't tell you how bad I was! I wished sometimes the waves 'ud wash me right off the ship, an' let me be drowned an' out of misery; for sick or well I had to do my work, and yer see I was new at it, an' clumsy, I 'spect, so I got more blows than kind words, you may be sure; an' the sailors hadn't a bit of pity; an' the way the captain used to swear at me was awful.

"I fair dreaded climbin' into the riggings sometimes, wi' my head all of a swim, an' the vessel a-rollin' till the yard-arms touched the sea, an' pitchin' an lurchin' all the while 'nough to bring yer heart up. But I had to do it.

"I had to take my turn wi' the watch, too, an' tumble out of my warm hammock an' struggle on deck jist when I'd got fair asleep.

"Talk about a sailor's life bein' pleasant! The

boys ought to be told better. You might as well be in a prison. I guess there's a sight more room to move about in in most gaols, an' quite as much change of company, an', very like, more change of diet; for when you've been out a month or six weeks the beef gets awful salt, and the hard tuck's mighty dry, an' the water poor enough, goodness knows.

"An' then, when the weather's foul, its misery: no sleep for nights on the stretch, an' in yer wet clothes all the while, till yer skin is fair blistered, an' yer eyes smartin' like coals of fire.

"Before I'd been to sea a fortnight, I wished myself well out of it, I can tell yer. An' I reckon it's the same wi' most boys, only they don't like to confess it, an' stick to it for shame of backin' out.

"Well, we were more'n seven weeks gettin' to New Brunswick. Weren't I glad to see land again, that's all! An' I was so sick of the sea, an' the wickedness of the sailors, an' the cuffs and kicks of the captain, that I'd made up my mind that, as soon as we got into port, I'd be off. 'No more sea for me,' says I. 'America is a big country, they say, an' I'll find somethink to do somewheres.'

"But no sich luck. I b'lieve the captain could read my thoughts; or very likely he guessed, after the treatment I'd got, I'd be off, so he took care not to give me the chance.

"Talk about sailors seein' the wonders of furren lands! I tell yer, all the time we was in port I never once set foot on shore. Never once. There's always somebody awake on board ship. An' there ain't the ghost of a chance of anybody slippin' off without bein'

S

seen.   I tried it once or twice,—an' a precious good
hidin' I got each time,—till I know'd it were no use;
so I giv'd up in despair.

"If I ever go to prison again, it shall be a prison
wi' stone walls.   No more timber gaols for me."

CHAPTER IX.

MORE TROUBLE.

" IT were in the middle of December —on a Wednesday, I mind it very well— when we left New Brunswick for Havre, with our hold stuffed nearly full of timber, an' a cargo on deck of the same sort.

"The weather was very fine, but the cold were a sneezer. Why, bless yer! at times we didn't know if we had any hands, or feet, or ears, or noses, or anythink, 't were that cold. An' then, when we begun to thaw a bit, it were like bein' roasted on a gridiron—the burnin' an' stingin' were jist awful.

" Folks as wants to know what cold is should spend a winter at sea, an' tackle a frozen sail on a' slippery rope, wi' a keen nor'-eastern blowing, an' yer fingers achin' up to the armpits—I guess one try 'ud satisfy 'em for the rest of their lives.

" Well, we didn't mind, the cold so much, so long as it kept fine. Down in the fokesel it were warm enough ; but it were precious hard work to turn out at three bells to relieve the watch, when the wind was keen enough to take all the skin off yer face.

" When we'd been out about a fortnight, however, the weather changed again, an' it weren't a change for the better either, an' day after day it got worse an' worse, an' the cold was a'most more than we could bear. Talk about it blowin' great guns ! I thought our outward passage were bad enough ; but this were a hundred times worse, while the snow an' hail comed down till we were fair blinded.

" The cold were bad enough when we were dry ; but think what it must ha' been when we were wet to the skin, an' great seas of icy-cold water breakin' over us, an' not a chance of gettin' below or snatchin' a mouthful of victuals ! It's bad enough to be wet when the weather is middlin' warm, but when yer clothes freeze round your body as stiff as boards, an' great patches of skin come off as big as sixpences—well, then it's a caution, I can tell yer.

" Well, the storm, instead of 'batin', got worse, if that were possible ; an' the sea !—well, I can't describe it, an' it's no use tryin'. The sight from the top of some of the great waves was awful. It were like a great stretch of barren country, wi' high hills an' deep valleys, but ever changin'——the hills sinkin' down, an' the valleys poppin' up; an' the anger of it were terrible to see!

"We hadn't much chance of reefin' some of the sails, for they were split into ribbons an' blown away. Then the deck cargo broke loose, an' stove the sky-lights in, an' the water rushed in like mad. We tried our best to keep it out, but 't weren't much use; an' afore dark our boxes and clothes were swimmin 'bout in the fokesel.

"We hadn't a chance of goin' below that night, any of us, for the pumps had to be kept a-goin' all the time, an' every hand was wanted.

"Afore mornin' the main top-gallant went with a crash, an' that were the signal for the others to go; an' we had to leave the pumps to cut away the riggin', that the vessel might right herself.

"We were glad enough to see the mornin', you may be sure. But it didn't bring no hope. The storm raged as wild as ever, an' the sea broke over us incessant; so that if we hadn't been well lashed we should ha' been washed away altogether.

"Soon after daylight the rudder went, an' we lay jist like a log——every wave breakin' over us. We had no fire, an' nothin' to cook if we had, for nearly all the ship's stores were spoiled wi' the salt water.

"The bumpin' of the logs in the hold, too, was by this time awful, an' we know'd very well that she were breakin' up. If she'd had any other kind of cargo she'd ha' gone to the bottom long afore.

"We should ha' taken to the boats if we had any,

but they had both been carried away wi' the masts; so there was nothin' to do but make a raft an' prepare for the worst.

"Well, we set to work, but we were all of us a'most dead wi' cold an' hunger. We hadn't much hope either that we'd ever be rescued; but for all that we seemed anxious-like to live as long as we could, or, as it seemed to me, make the death-struggle last out.

"However, we worked away at the raft. It took away our thoughts a bit from death, an' it were exercise, too, an' kept us from being froze quite up. But it were no joke to tie a raft up, wi' the waves breakin' over us incessant.

"We didn't finish it a bit too soon, neither. For hours the *Nora* 'd been lurchin' and strugglin' as if she'd nearly lost heart too, an' couldn't keep up much longer. Then all of a sudden the wind shifted an' caught her a broadside. We feels her a-heelin' over, an' we gets on the raft, none too soon; over she turns on her side, an' we floats away afore the wind.

"But what we suffered nobody 'll never know; for no words can tell it, an' I don't b'lieve anybody 'll ever be able to think it. Was you ever at sea in a storm, sir?"

"Yes, Mike."

"But not on a raft, I guess?"

"No."

"Well, then, I'll never be able to make it clear to you. I can't think how we kept from bein' washed off the thing, an' how we suffered the cold an' lived is beyond me altogether. All through that awful night, wi' the water a-surgin' up between the logs, and the freezin' wind a-hissin' past, I prayed to the good Lord to have mercy on us; an' the sailors prayed too, an' the captain an' all. There weren't no swearin' on the raft, I can tell you, for you see death was lookin' us straight in the eyes all the time.

"Durin' the night the wind went down a very great deal, an next day 't was moderate calm; so I was told after. But I don't remember nothin' about that day, after seein' the day break. I mind seein' that very well, and then, seems to me, I dropped asleep.

"When I comed-to, I was for long enough afore I could make out where I was, or what had come to me : I was in sich a nice berth, wi' clean white sheets an' the air all so warm round me. Well, I kept a-wonderin' an' wonderin' where I was for ever so long; but at last a gentleman comed up to the side of my berth and told me.

"I was on board one of the Allan steamers, he said, and he were the doctor; and we had been taken off a raft in Mid Atlantic; an' that one of the sailors were quite dead, an' one had died since, an' that I were very ill, an' he were afraid I'd never come round.

"He seemed mighty pleased, too, when he found I were able to talk; an' he *were* kind, an' couldn't ha' been more gentle wi' me if he had been my mother. Well, when the vessel reach'd Liverpool I were brought here—that's three weeks ago—an' here I've been ever since.

" I've suffered a powerful deal, too, since I've been here——I was frostbitten so badly, and that's like being scalded; but my feet were the worst. Poor old feet! You see I've lost 'em both."

" Yes, Mike, so the nurse told me. I'm very sorry for you."

" Oh, but I'm not goin' to be any more down-hearted than I can help," he said with a smile. " You remember I told you I were gettin' new understandin'?"

" Yes, Mike."

" So, yer see, I'll be on a new footin' when I get about again. The doctor says as how cork-feet won't look at all bad, an', wi' practice, I'll be able to walk very fair."

" I am glad you are able to look on the bright side of things, Mike."

" Well, what's the use of lookin' any other side?" was the cheerful answer. 'I've had need to look the bright side, I can tell yer, for I've had a fairish bit to go through. Don't yer think so?"

" You have, indeed!"

" But I guess the worst is over now. I shan't go to sea no more, that's certain. An' she says " (with a grateful look in the direction of the lady already spoken of) " as how I can be a tailor or a shoemaker. I think I'd rather make shoes, though; that was father's trade."

Here the lady—who was nurse at the Royal Southern Hospital in which Mike lay—came forward, and Mike welcomed her with a face of sunshine.

" I've brought you some jelly, Mike," she said gently. " Do you think you can manage it?"

"Oh, yes, lady!" he said brightly—he always called her lady. "I'm gettin' a famous appetite!"

"You're a brave boy!" she said, with a sweet smile lighting up her face. "But now I think you'd better give over talking, and see if you cannot eat."

Poor Mike! He evidently did his best, but his will was greater than his ability; and we were sorry to see that most of the delicacies brought to him were taken away again untouched.

CHAPTER X.

REST.

ON my next visit to the hospital, "Lady" met me at the foot of the stairs.

I may as well adopt the name by which Mike always addressed her, for surely no name could be more appropriate. Not only was she a lady by virtue of education and social position, but also by virtue of that instinctive refinement and gentleness which made her life a benediction, and her face a vision of peace.

Lady's face, however, wore a troubled expression to-day, and scarcely had I taken her outstretched hand when she said,—

"Poor little Mike is dying."

"Dying!" I repeated in some astonishment; I am sorry to hear that."

" And I am sorry," she said, " for I have got to love the little fellow almost as though he were my own. Any one so sweet and patient as he has been I never knew."

" And is there no hope for him ? "

" None. What the doctor most feared has happened."

" And what is that ? "

" Mortification."

" And does he know ? "

" No, poor child ; he thinks he is better ; for of course all the pain has left him now, and he lies there quite happy."

" Poor little fellow."

" This morning, almost as soon as it was day, I heard him singing, ever so sweetly :

> ' Give to the winds thy fears,
> Hope and be undismayed.' "

" That was one of his mother's favourite hymns, he told me."

" Yes. She must have been a brave, sweet woman, for her life has left a beautiful impression upon his heart. But I wanted your opinion. Had we better tell him, think you, that he is dying ? "

" I think not. No good could come of it, and I think it would be better to let the little fellow dream himself away into the other and better life."

" Yes, perhaps you are right. You will be pleased to hear that we have succeeded at length in finding his friend Gracey, and we expect her here this afternoon."

" And does Mike know ? "

" No ; I thought we had better not tell him, lest

she should fail to come, and then the disappointment would be so great."

" I hope she will come, for it will cheer the little fellow's heart to see his old friend."

" Yes! He often wonders if she is still living."

.   .   .   .   .   .

Mike's welcome was as genial as ever, though the shake of his hand was feebler than it had wont to be; and ever and anon there came into his eyes a dreamy, sleepy expression, which too surely betokened the last long sleep that was swiftly coming upon him.

" And how are you to-day, Mike ? "

" Well," he answered, rousing himself and speaking slowly, " I thought I were better this mornin'; but now "———

" And what now, Mike ? " we said, after a long pause.

He smiled faintly as he answered, " Now I think I'm goin' to God ! "

" What makes you think that ? " we asked.

" Well," he answered, " I don't know as how I can make it very plain ; but I don't feel as if I have any grip of anythink, as I had. When the pain left me early this morin' I thought I were goin' to git better right off ; but since then I've got to feel dull an' strange, an' my eyes keep seein' things that ain't here, an' my thoughts a-wandering off all sorts of ways. Do you make it out ? "

" Yes, I think so."

" There's a wall there wi' pictures on it, ain't there ? "

" Yes, Mike."

" Well, I've only to look at it for a moment or so an' it all goes away—melts off like ; an' I see the country stretchin' away for miles an' miles. Sich beautiful country, too! wi' the grass so green an' smooth, an' the hills covered with trees, an' flowers growin' everywhere, and clear streams of water windin' in an' out, and people walkin' up an' down, an' childer —oh, sich heaps of 'em!—lookin' as happy as anythink. An' the longer I look the plainer it gets; an' I could almost be sartin that I seen mother and little May there."

"And do you see the country now, Mike?"

"Aye," he said, smiling winsomely. "I've been trying to look at you, but you melt away like everythink else. An' away out there—you don't see it, maybe—is sich a beautiful garden. I reckon I'll go an' walk in it by an by."

"Will you be sorry to go, Mike?"

The question seemed to call him back from dreamland, and he looked at us with a fixed expression for a moment or two.

"No," he answered, speaking slowly. "No, I think I'll be glad. You see I've no feet now, an' I'd be a cripple all the days of my life; an' I'd have to struggle very hard, an' be very poor, an' have to live in a cellar, p'r'aps, an' never git a sight of the country or a smell of the flowers. No, I'm not sorry. They're all out there—father an' mother an' May. I'm all alone here, an' have no feet; an' it's very hard to be alone an' a cripple. No, I'll be glad to go. Mother 'll be lookin' out for me, I reckon; an' May,—bless her little heart!—she'll be mighty glad to have me wi' her again. An' I guess I'll have new feet there; better than cork ones. An' I won't be tired any more, or hungry, or cold. No, I'm not sorry. I think I'll be very glad."

When he ceased speaking, his eyes caught again that dreamy, far-away look that was rarely absent now. And around the corners of his mouth happy smiles kept playing hide-and-seek.

He looked up again after a while, and said,—

" Maybe you won't mind readin' to me a bit ? "

So we read to him parts of his favourite chapter :

" And He showed me a pure river of water of life, clear as crystal, proceeding out of the throne of God and of the Lamb.

" In the midst of the street of it, and on either side of the river, was there the Tree of Life, which bare twelve manner of fruits, and yielded her fruits every month ; and the leaves of the tree were for the healing of the nations.

" And there shall be no more curse ; but the throne of God and of the Lamb shall be in it ; and His servants shall serve Him.

" And they shall see His face, and His name shall be in their foreheads.

" And there shall be no night there, and they need no candle, neither light of the sun ; for the Lord God giveth them light ; and they shall reign for ever and ever."

He did not seem to heed when we had done reading. He lay with closed eyes, and with his hands clasped above the coverlet. But it needed no doctor to tell that the tide of his brief and stormy life was ebbing fast.

A sweet boyish face it was that lay there on the

white pillow, placid now as the dying of a summer's day. After the storm and tumult, rest had come. No shadow of care could we trace on the pale forehead; no line of pain about the gentle mouth. He lay there in the quiet of the eventide, waiting for the opening of the gates.

How long we might have watched him we know not; but just then we caught the sound of a quick footstep on the floor behind us. Mike heard it also, for he opened his eyes with a start. The next moment a little wrinkled woman brushed quickly past us, and, with a glad cry from Mike, " Oh, Gracey, Gracey ! " the two were locked in each other's arms.

. . . . . .

What passed between them we cannot tell. We left them together; and Gracey remained with him till the last.

" There was no need," Lady said to me the following day, " that any one should tell him. He knew almost as soon as we did that he was dying. And glad enough he was to go. It seemed easy, gentle dying, too. If the poor boy's day was stormy, the evening was without a cloud. A happier face than his, as the end grew near, one could not imagine; and not an hour before he passed away I heard him singing to Gracey a snatch from an old hymn :

> " ' This the hope that shall sustain me,
> Till life's pilgrimage be past :
> Fears may vex and troubles pain me,
> I shall reach my home at last.' "

He passed away like a child falling asleep. We saw

no dying ; we only knew at last that poor little **Mike** was dead.

. . . . .

There were sick and suffering yet to be visited ; and as I entered the ward where Mike's bright smile had so often greeted me, I instinctively looked in the direction of his bed, but it was empty now. And then only did I realize that my gentle little friend had passed away from the shadows of earth to the land where there is no more suffering, and no more death.

THE END.

PRINTED BY MORRISON AND GIBB LIMITED, EDINBURGH